DATE DUE			
MAY 1 1			
MAY 1 8			
OCT 2 1973			
OCT 2 2 1973			
NOV 2 9 1973			
DEC 1 2 1973			
JAN 1 7 1974			
FEB 1 9 1974			
APR. 8			
APR. 1 6 1975			
MAY 3			
MAY 1 6			
MAR. 19 APR 1 1976			
			63

So Great A Love

By GLADYS MALVERN

For pretty Hal Wade, lady-in-waiting to King Charles I's vivacious French wife, the English world has always seemed a simple and pleasant place, with the gracious and fun-loving noblemen and the serious, stolid folk of low degree alike contented with their lives. How, then, have Oliver Cromwell's sour-faced Puritans gained so much popular support that Parliament can wage war against the King, a brave gentleman who insists only on his God-given rights? When handsome, heart-stirring Jerry Vane, grandson of the Wades' housekeeper, comes back from his studies at Oxford a crop-haired firebrand of a Roundhead, Hal finds herself not only attracted but disturbed by his bold, admiring glances, for she is of noble birth and inescapably betrothed to the middle-aged Duke of Thewes.

"Duty and Loyalty" is the Wade family motto, and duty has always come easily to Hal, dressing in silks and satins, playing games and attending to the light conversations and flirtations of court life. Even after the King and his Royalists have taken to fighting the surly Parliamentarians in field and hedgerow and the valiant Queen has to play hide and seek for her life in castles and huts all over England, Hal finds fate puzzling but her own role clear. However, when Jerry turns up again, a Puritan hero, with the Queen and her court at his mercy, Hal's sense of social values faces a shocking challenge. Her loyalty dictates one line of duty and her emotions quite another: now she must make a choice between her Queen and social heritage and a heart's desire that can no longer be denied.

So Great A Love

by Gladys Malvern

 MACRAE SMITH COMPANY: PHILADELPHIA

contents

So Great A Love

1 ❁

the mounting menace

LADY HENRIETTA WADE SLEPT LATE ON THAT BRIGHT NOVEMber morning in 1641, awakening with the pleasant awareness that this was her off-duty day. In the big, canopied four-poster, high and soft with sweetly scented feather mattresses, she stretched luxuriously, thankful that the morning was sunny and asking herself whether she should wear the green satin or the new cerise velvet.

When her two maids entered, one carrying a tray with her breakfast, she greeted them cheerily.

"Good morning, my lady," one of them replied. "Her Majesty wishes to see you at your earliest convenience."

"Oh!" She sat up, conscious of a sense of alarm. "On my off day? It must be something of tremendous importance."

It was almost a year since she had taken her mother's place as lady-in-waiting to her Majesty, Queen Henrietta Maria, known to the people of England as Queen Mary. Henrietta had been named for the Queen, who had stood as godmother at her baptism seventeen years ago.

Soon after this spoiled, temperamental princess, then sixteen, had come to England to marry Charles I, she had found a firm friend in Anne Wade, Marchioness of Langdon, whom the young King had appointed as one of her ladies.

After his Majesty had dismissed his bride's French retinue, the young Queen had drawn close to the Marchioness, perhaps because Anne Wade spoke French so fluently and at that time the Queen had known no English. A year ago when the illness of the Marchioness forced her retirement from court, the Queen had happily accepted her daughter as her substitute.

Lady Hal and Queen Mary had grown genuinely fond of one another during this trying year when the royal couple had been confronted with one annoyance after another, their cares mounting daily.

As a child, Henrietta had been nicknamed Henry. Then this, too, had been shortened until now she was called Hal. With her gaiety, optimism and devotion she was often able to divert Queen Mary from her incessant tribulations and worries, and once the Queen, who spoke English with a French accent, exclaimed to her adoring husband, "Ah, *ma foi!* What would I do without my petite Hal! So decorative, so full to overflowing with life, always so sweet and understanding. I love her as if she were my own daughter. She is one person I can trust."

"What now?" thought Hal as she finished her breakfast and hurriedly began to dress to answer the royal summons. "What new vexation for her Majesty? The green satin, Moll, and slippers to match. The emeralds."

Finally she was ready—a slender, graceful figure of medium height in a floor-length gown of heavy, gleaming satin, its neckline wide and low in the current mode, with puffed, elbow-length sleeves.

To look at her, so bright and lively, one would think she

had nothing more on her mind than a new costume for a masquerade or the learning of a part in one of the plays by Ben Jonson, Beaumont or Fletcher which were frequently produced at court. But these were serious times in England and since the Queen had summoned her on one of her free days, it must be because of something gravely important.

"Whatever can it be?"

Despite the trouble with Parliament, until a month ago life at court had assumed an outer air of gaiety. There were masquerades, plays produced—sometimes by professionals but usually by members of the court—concerts, quoits, tennis, archery contests, hawking, hunting, backgammon, chess, cards, bowling, dicing—always something amusing going on; but lately the court had been a dull place, for the King and Queen found it more and more difficult to disguise their worry, and every courtier, too, acknowledged that the situation was grave, what with the King and Parliament always quarreling, and those absurd, narrow-minded Puritans growing stronger day by day.

As far back as the time of Elizabeth the Puritans had been persecuted and Elizabeth had done her best to stamp out this troublesome sect, but they had met clandestinely and grown all the stronger. As Hal moved quickly along the corridor toward the Queen's apartment she thought that if there was one thing in this world she hated it was those preposterous Puritans.

In sharp contrast to the Puritans, the Cavaliers—Royalists—were a pleasure-loving, sportive sort, dressing luxuriously, gambling, dancing and singing, devotees of the theater. Not that they were insincere religionists. They belonged to the Church of England, kept fast days and worshipped in their ornate chapels. But the Puritans! They dressed plainly and in dull colors, and clipped their hair

11

close, so that they were called Roundheads. To them the theater was "the devil's workshop" and everything that brought merriment they labeled a sin.

"Heaven preserve us from those dreadful Puritans!" Hal muttered. "If only the whole lot of them would migrate to the colonies!"

She had reached the entrance to the Queen's sitting room now, and she was a refreshing picture as she knelt—a slim, girlish figure with a delicately oval face, light-brown hair with glints of gold in it; dark, vivacious eyes with extraordinarily long lashes, and a soft, beautiful mouth.

The Queen was alone in the huge, ornate room with her small dog Mitte, her pet monkey named Pug, and her favorite dwarf, Jeffrey Hudson. Hudson was a perfectly formed little man, richly dressed in pale blue velvet with a wide white collar edged with lace. Mary was excessively fond of these small persons and usually had several around her, but Jeffrey Hudson was more intelligent than the others and he adored the Queen.

Mary, now in her early thirties, was a beautiful woman. Her shiny black hair was carefully coiffed in the French style called *tête de mouton,* with numerous frizzed curls. She was slight and graceful, and her slender face with its delicate and well-balanced features looked at least five years younger than her age.

Her black eyes were lively, keen and expressive, sometimes flashing with anger, for she had a high temper; but usually she was a sweet and sympathetic mistress to those who served her. She lived under the disadvantage of knowing herself to be hated by her husband's people, who resented the fact that their king had married a Catholic and permitted his wife openly to practice her religion. She was especially detested by the Roundheads, who accused her, and rightly, of influencing the King to stand fast in his resolve to retain the unlimited power of an absolute monarch.

Mary set her ladies a high standard in the matter of dress. She had the true French flair for tasteful attire and today her gown was of lustrous satin with the modish full skirt and wide ruffles of sheer lace cascading from her elbow-length sleeves.

"*Bon jour, ma chérie,*" she said smilingly. "Come, we'll sit down. Jeffrey, take Pug off the sofa and make Mitte be quiet! Always he growls, that one."

"Good morning, your Majesty. Has something new happened to cause the Queen's Grace more anxiety? I was thinking as I walked down the hall, those dreadful Puritans——"

"*Non, ma petite.* This time it is another matter. This morning I received a letter from your *chère maman.* I am sorry to hear that she is not improving. She says she is worse."

"Oh!"

"She asks my leave for you to go to her. Your good papa, Monsieur le Marquess, has also received a letter from her and will return with you. You will both leave this afternoon. Ah, I hope you find her better!"

"I'm sorry my mother is worse. Until now I haven't worried about her, since the doctor assured us that her illness wasn't fatal and I know she's well cared for. But it grieves me to leave you, madam, especially now when you have so much to trouble you and more than ever you need to be surrounded by friends."

"*Parbleu! C'est vrai.* Every day it grows worse. I shall miss you, Hal. *Ma foi,* I love you almost as much as my own daughters, but to keep you here would be selfish." In a

13

quick, spontaneous gesture she reached out and grasped Hal's hands. "But come back to me so soon you can—wherever I may be. I do not command you now. I implore you."

"Of course I shall return, but—wherever you may be, madam? This is a strange phrase. Where would the Queen's Grace be but with the King in one of his palaces?"

Mary's eyes grew stark with dread. "These days, *ma chère,* one can never tell. *Entre nous,* I might have to—to leave England."

"Oh, no, madam! No, never. It will never come to that!"

Mary gave an expressive French shrug. "Wherever I am, you come to me. *Eh bien, c'est entendu.* God go with you. I understand the roads are no longer safe, especially for people known to have association with his Majesty. *Mon Dieu,* why—why should the commoners hate us so?"

"It's an animosity fostered by that hateful Parliament."

"*Oui.* But we'll talk no more of that." Mary smiled pensively. "Give to your dear *maman* my love. Tell her I hope soon to see her. And now, *au revoir, chérie,* and remember, come back to me—wherever I am!"

Disturbed by the Queen's intensity, Hal nodded. "I promise. *Adieu,* madam. God keep you well and safe. With your Majesty's permission I will go now and get ready for the journey."

"*Oui. Certainement.*"

The Queen kissed her, then Hal knelt again, rose and backed out of the room. How odd and terrible that their Majesties should be undergoing this direful feeling of insecurity! Surely it must be baseless, for what in all the world could be more stable than the throne of England?

Returning to her own room, Hal ordered her two maids to start packing. Though worried about her mother, she did not feel that the Marchioness was in danger of death. The doctor had said that she would be an invalid for the rest of her life but that she would probably live for a long time.

As Hal stood watching the maids pack her jewelry and her lovely dresses, her father entered—a short, rotund man, elaborately garbed in a white satin doublet with pale green velvet breeches, with his long, shoulder-length hair parted in the middle and artificially waved. His rapierlike sword with an ornamental hilt hung from his belt. His face was long rather than round, a good-natured, somewhat ruddy face, with the fashionable mustache and pointed chin beard, always neatly trimmed. His eyes were small, blue and twinkly. He had the suggestion of a paunch. Hal curtsied respectfully.

"I see the Queen has informed you that we leave this afternoon," he observed in his hearty way. "Would two of the clock be too soon for you? We shall stop at Oxford where George will join us."

"Father, what did Mother say in her letter to you? She must be very much worse or she wouldn't have sent for us."

"It seems she is experiencing a slight setback, no doubt due to her intense worriment over the deplorable condition of the country; but she confesses that she is unbearably lonely without us and in her letter to the Queen she made her condition worse than it actually is in order that we might all be together at Christmas. We're fortunate in having such an excellent woman as Cheam to take care of her. Ah, these are troublous times, Hal. The contest between the King and Parliament is like a boiling kettle. The lid is apt to blow off at any moment."

"What do you mean?"

"I mean," he said, his voice low and his eyes grave, "that there is apt to be war."

15

"War! Oh, no! War between the King and his people? Civil war? That's unthinkable! What loyal Englishman would take up arms against the crown?"

"How else can this matter be settled? Odds fish! One must either be on the side of Parliament or on the side of the King. His Majesty will die rather than give in. Oh, it's no new thing, this state of affairs. I remember his father, King James, was always struggling with Parliament, always resisting its intention to make laws and fix taxes. It's a deplorable condition that Charles has inherited. To my mind Parliament is a pack of blundering, traitorous, rascally upstarts. Like his father, Charles insists that he rules by divine right."

"Why, so he does!" exclaimed Hal. "Who dares doubt it?"

"The whole country is doubting it. Depend upon it, Hal, Charles will never acquiesce to Parliament's demands. He's a fine, honorable man, a far better man than his father was, but he has the Scotch stubbornness in him. He's ready to fight for his principles—and fight he'll have to! So now you see why your mother, sizing up the situation, wants her family with her."

"He'd take up arms against his own people? Oh, Father, no! It won't come to that. Surely, surely, it won't come to that! It can't happen. What's a king for if not to rule? How can a king be little more than a puppet?"

"True, my dear. The King, be he good or bad, has always ruled, but our world is changing. That rule is being challenged. God alone knows what lies in store for us all. Well, be ready promptly at two."

He walked out of the room and Hal went to the window, staring moodily into the quiet garden below. Civil war! The idea was bewildering and frightening. Civil war. The King

16

against his own people, the people against their King. It was fantastic. What could happen to prevent it? Nothing—unless Parliament backed down from its arrogant position —for, knowing Charles Stuart, she realized that he would never surrender his right to govern. No, not one iota.

True, as her father had said, the trouble had been brewing for a long time.

When Elizabeth had died without heirs in 1603, James had been summoned from Scotland to take her place on England's throne, thus becoming James I. During the twenty-two years of his reign he and Parliament had engaged in incessant bickerings, for even then Parliament had been determined to lessen the power of the throne.

In 1625 when James had died and his stalwart son became Charles I at the age of twenty-five, the difficulties increased. England, fanatically Protestant, had been resentful when the new King had flaunted popular opinion and married a Catholic princess. Because of her religion the Queen had always been unpopular. Her very presence added to the grievances of a restive and determined populace. It was she, they said—and rightly—who goaded the King into taking so firm a stand. But for her a compromise might have been achieved. The people were convinced that her power over the King, who loved her madly, was to blame for bringing this conflict to the point of explosion.

Like all staunch Royalists, Hal was convinced that Parliament was wrong in its presumptuous insistence that it, and not the King, should levy taxes and manage both foreign and domestic affairs. In her opinion government belonged solely to the King, and the King was fully justified in fighting anyone who dared challenge his supreme authority.

Such an attitude was inbred in Henrietta Wade. Always

her ancestors had been courtiers. Though personally dis-
liking James, the Marquess of Langdon had served him
loyally, for according to the Wade code, though you might
not respect the King, you must reverence the throne and
fight if need be to maintain it.

The Wades heartily approved of Charles as a man. Tall,
strong, well-built, he was decent, intelligent, well-meaning,
devoted to his wife and family, loyal to his friends, naturally
kind and courageous, and honestly desiring to be a good
ruler; yet from the beginning his reign had been one of
incessant turmoil.

In 1628 Parliament had dared to put forth what it termed
the "Petition of Right" which restricted the power of the
King. Majestically, Charles had dismissed this Parliament
and for the next eleven years he had called no other into
session. The people grumbled, but submitted.

Then in 1638 Charles, who was also King of Scotland
through his grandmother, the tragic Mary, Queen of Scots,
had tried to impose his idea of religion upon the hardy,
turbulent Scots, for he could not understand how any
people would presume to worship as they chose.

Though the Protestant Church was the national church
of Scotland, he was determined that henceforth the Scots
must renounce this and adhere to the teaching and the rites
of the Church of England. The Scots rose up in open revolt
and to Charles there was only one thing to do—fight them
and so bring them into submission. Thinking about that
now, Hal grudgingly admitted that perhaps in this the King
had been wrong.

Anyhow, in order to fight the Scots, Charles had to have
an army and in order to maintain and equip an army he
had to impose more taxes upon his already overburdened
subjects. Consequently, last year—November, 1640—in

order to raise funds, he had been compelled to summon into session another Parliament.

When this group met it was in no mood for appeasement. It was arbitrary, reckless and determined. Boldly it announced that whether summoned by his Majesty or not, it intended to meet every three years. The Royalists had been aghast at this defiant pronouncement. The King and Queen had been coldly furious.

And now it seemed that matters were rapidly approaching a climax. How and when would it end? To Hal's mind the conflict could end in only one way—complete triumph for the King. Then everything would be safe and normal again.

She noticed that her maids had finished packing and that some menservants had entered to take her boxes downstairs to be placed in a wagon.

"My lady, do you care to change your dress?" asked one of the maids.

Hal nodded and they helped her into a riding habit, its waist tight-fitting and its velvet skirt especially designed for the sidesaddle. Over this splendid, sweeping garment she would wear a flowing, ermine-lined cape. Her modish hat had a high crown and a waving plume. How dreadful it would be, she mused, surveying herself in the mirror, how dreadful it would be to be a Puritan! No plumes, no rouge, no jewels, no fetching hats, no bright, becoming colors, no perfume. Why, they considered it sinful for a woman to look pretty! Imagine!

Lunch was served at a small table near the mullioned window—a substantial meal of boiled mutton with caper sauce, a broiled lark, a huge mug of cider, bread, salad, cheese, an apple tart and a quince pie. As she was finishing, a letter was handed to her.

Breaking the seal, she read, frowning at the news:

To Lady Henrietta Wade from his grace William Tamerskey, Duke of Thewes.

My esteemed and illustrious lady:

I regretfully inform your ladyship that I have suddenly been called to France on business. The date of my return is uncertain, but I have informed the Marquess, your father, that I may be reached at . . .

She crumpled the paper and tossed it in the fire. What did she care where the man could be reached? Certainly, she would never try to reach him! She hoped he would stay in France forever.

This was another irksome matter to add to her sense of discomfort. The Duke. Girls in her position were rarely consulted as to whom they would marry. Her father had been vastly proud when six months ago he had been approached by the Duke requesting a plight-troth to his daughter. There was no better match in England. The Duke was a widower and enormously rich. True, he was fat, pompous and in his early fifties, but an easygoing sort, sure to treat his young wife indulgently. No date had been set for the wedding, the Marquess pleading his daughter's youth and her desire to have a year of freedom at court.

When told of this arrangement Hal had been incensed. True, a lady of her rank could not expect to marry for love. It was her duty to accept her father's choice.

"But he's so old," she expostulated, "and so fat!"

"What do you expect, an Adonis? Come, my dear, I thought you'd be delighted. Married to him, you'll have precedence over most of the women at court."

Watching the note as it was caught by the flames, she

said to herself that the Duke had gone to France because he was afraid. He foresaw trouble and rather than be called to risk his life for the King, he had manufactured an excuse to get out of England to a safer place. Yes, the man was a coward, and she would plead with her father to break this troth!

She scarcely knew this man. She had never been alone with him and he had never so much as kissed her hand, but she knew he was a bore and she knew that never, never would she love him.

Love. Would she ever know what love really was? How glorious a thing it would be if she could one day love a man as the Queen loved Charles! But perhaps that was too much to ask. And certainly, her Majesty had not loved Charles when she had married him.

A manservant entered and bowed. "The Marquess is waiting in the forecourt, my lady."

"Yes. I am ready."

As she rose, a maid put the cape about her shoulders, while another handed her her gauntlets with their wide, richly embroidered cuffs. Then Hal paused, gazing pensively about the ornate room and the thought came to her that she might never see it again. She sighed and turned toward the door.

In the courtyard her two maids were already climbing into the wagon, warmly hooded against the brisk November breeze. Standing on either side of her father were his valet and secretary, while a short distance off, mounted, were about a hundred horsemen, her father's own men, who would serve as protectors on the long journey.

A groom assisted her to mount and respectfully handed her a small whip. So they started off, she and her father riding side by side at a sprightly pace, the servants and the luggage cart in the rear, the men at arms divided—half preceding the party, half following it.

It was good to be going home, she thought, for she loved the house in which she had been born—Langdon Hall, near Shottery. Though not among the great castles of England, it was certainly one of the most beautiful.

London was a busy, noisy and smelly place—odorous because the streets were used as sewers. There were a few coaches, a vehicle used only in the city, since as yet no one had thought to equip them with springs, and they were uncomfortable for long journeys. Among the coaches moved the richly appareled horsemen and the sedan chairs; and venders darted about recklessly, hawking their wares, each one trying to outshout the others.

"Fresh eggs. Fresh eggs here!"

"Milk here. Good, fresh milk."

"Fine mousetraps here!"

"Suffolk cheese. Butter, three pence a pound!"

"Herrings. Two for a groat. Get your plump herrings!"

"White-hearted cabbages!"

"Oysters? Oysters?"

"Hot, fine oatcakes!"

"Hot codlins and pies here!"

"Lily white vinegar!"

"Ol' clothes. Any ol' clothes for sale?"

It all seemed reassuringly normal: signs creaking in the wind; carts; the smoke from the breweries; the sound of horses' hoofs on the narrow, cobbled streets; ragged chimney sweeps with blackened faces; women with market baskets; people going about their business seemingly devoid of rebellious notions.

"Did the Queen tell you," asked the Marquess in a low

voice, "that she was making secret plans to escape if need be?"

"She hinted as much. That was what she meant when she made me promise to come to her wherever she might be."

"I remember when I went to France with the Duke of Buckingham to escort her to England. I thought I had never seen a more beautiful—watch out! That woman's about to throw some slops from that upper window!"

They managed to avoid the odorous downpour, and when they had turned into another street Hal's father spoke angrily. "She did that on purpose, suspecting that we were from court! Probably one of those grim, ill-mannered Puritans. Odds fish, how they hate us!"

London no longer seemed normal. Hal could scarcely wait to get out of it.

2 ✿

the way home

OXFORD, STATELY AND QUIET, RECEIVED THE MARQUESS AND
his daughter with courtesy. As they passed in the street,
people removed their hats, bowed and made room for them
politely, and when they stopped at an inn they were given
excellent service. For the Royalists, Oxford was a charming
oasis in that turbulent realm, being staunchly and proudly
pro-Cavalier. The male inhabitants of this beautiful town
wore their hair long to their shoulders and curled at the
tips, not closely cut in the Puritan, or Roundhead, style
which Hal considered ugly and ridiculous.

In their pleasant rooms, while she and her father waited
for her brother, who was a student at Oxford, she took the
first opportunity to discuss her engagement.

"Father, I've been thinking——"

"There's much to think about these days, my dear."

"About my troth. I beg you, sir, I beg you to break it!"

Had she announced that she had turned Puritan, he
could not have been more astonished. "What? Are you
serious? This is nonsense, utter nonsense. Where would I

find a better match for you? Tell me that. The Duke of Thewes is——"

"I know all that is said about him, but the fact is, I don't love him and having become slightly better acquainted with him since the marriage contract was signed, I'm sure I never shall."

"Pouff. Romantic balderdash. Your mother and I weren't fond of one another, either, when we were betrothed, but now we get along right well."

"Father, please. I——"

"Is there someone else who has taken your fancy?"

"No. It isn't that. Father, don't scowl at me. The truth is, I want to love. I want to know how it feels to be really, desperately, wondrously in love."

"My dear, true love comes with association, mutual interests and understanding. Believe me, child, I'm speaking from experience."

Her dark eyes flashed rebelliously. "I won't marry the Duke!"

His frown deepened. "Won't? Dare you speak that way to your father? Come now, are you part of this universal defiance? Is it contagious? A contract is a contract. A plight-troth, you know, is no light thing to be broken because of the whim of a flighty, sentimental girl. You're young and romantic. Left to yourself, doubtless you'd choose some young and handsome rascal without a ha'penny to his name, some commoner who would woo you like a poet."

"No," she answered firmly, "I despise commoners. I'm not a fool. I know I was born to a certain estate and I've no desire to lower it. In fact, I'd like to elevate it, but——"

"Then the Duke's your man. Are you angry with him because he's off to France without first pleading with me to name the day?"

"I don't care enough about him to be angry with him. I hope he never comes back! Please, Father, sweet Father, write to him. Tell him—oh, tell him anything—but break this troth!"

"Don't 'sweet Father' me. You were agreeable enough to it when I proposed it to you."

"I had scarcely met him then. Besides, it was six months ago. I'm older now."

"It's not a light thing to break a troth. In fact, you ought to know that it cannot be done except by mutual agreement. And what excuse would I give? That my daughter is a flibbertigibbet with silly, romantic notions?"

"Oh, find some better reason—anything!"

"If we were poor, if I had lost all my money, I daresay his grace would agree to a breach of the contract, but otherwise—no, no, no. Let us have no further discussion about this. Instead of being dissatisfied, you should be proud that so eligible a man as the Duke of Thewes wishes to honor you by making you his duchess. Women! Odds fish, you think you are doing the best you can for them and they come a-pouting and a-pestering and having no sensible reason for their displeasure! You need not look at me in that reproachful way. The thing is settled!"

She opened her mouth to reply, but before she could speak, the door was flung open and George rushed into the room, embracing his father and sister with characteristic warmth.

At Langdon Hall there was a portrait painted of the Marquess when he was twenty, just George's age, and it seemed to Hal that except for the clothes it might have been a picture of George himself. Though far from stout, George was one of those small-boned men who would become so when he grew older. He did not wear the chin beard, but there was a slender, debonair mustache, carefully clipped, that gave him a certain sportive air. His hair was long and shiny and slightly darker than his sister's, and he was something of a dandy in his yellow satin doublet, blue cloak—full-cut and swirling—and yellow-lined, tight-fitting blue breeches and white shoes with red heels.

"So, you're taking me home, eh?" he asked gaily when the greetings were over. "You've decided that I've had sufficient education and I heartily concur. Farewell to books, to pompous teachers, to boring classes and tedious routines!"

"We're going home because Mother is worse," said Hal.

"Much worse?"

"No," replied the Marquess reassuringly. "I judge by her last letter that she is deeply concerned over conditions. Home to her seems a safe place for us to be, but actually, if there's war no place in England will be truly safe."

"War?" asked George, all levity abandoned. "Do you really think it will come to that, Father?"

"I am in the King's confidence. I know how worried he is, how tense—and I know him. He will never yield to the demands of Parliament. He should not! He should give these people the thrashing they deserve for their impertinence and audacity!"

"But actual war?" asked George. "Civil war? Could it possibly come to that?"

"What other way is there?" demanded his father, annoyed by the mere question. "Parliament wants its own power to be uppermost. It wants the King to reign with only a limited power, giving to them the supreme control. But mark me, the King is of no mind to relinquish his scepter. He is determined to rule Parliament, to be—as he terms it—'really King.' And if the worst comes to the worst, son, you and I must be ready to fight and possibly to die for him. In the long history of the Wade family its men have always rallied to the King's cause."

"Oh, absolutely, sir."

"I'm glad you feel that way, George. Meanwhile, it will be good to get home, to find quietness for a while."

Hal looked at them lovingly, her big eyes glittering with apprehension. The thought that either of them might be killed was unbearable. "It mustn't happen," she murmured. "Oh, please God, it mustn't happen!"

George laughed. "Girls! Why are the wenches so emotional? Look at her. In another moment she'll be in tears. Why are tears always so close with girls? The slightest word and they start blubbering. Be that as it may, I love them all, Puritan or princess, if they're pretty I love to look at them —soft and round and utterly bewitching."

She frowned at him. "Puritans! Don't even mention the creatures. I'd as soon be caught dead as associate with them. Prim, gloomy, self-righteous! A plague on Puritans!"

"I've seen some right pretty Puritans," answered her brother lightly. "But on the whole, I admit I prefer a girl who thinks it no sin to use a bit of rouge and a bit of perfume. I like my girls to be frilly and not too clever, if you please, and no taller than I."

His father laughed, rang for the servant and ordered what he considered a simple meal. Oysters, baked salmon, roast goose, broiled partridge, some cabbage and carrots, a cress salad, hot apple tarts, a dish of figs, warm bread and a round of cheese.

Breakfast at sunrise next morning was equally hearty, and as soon as they finished it they were off. The weather had turned blustery and the sun was overcast. At the swift pace they took, they would reach Langdon Hall in three days. The somnolent village of Shottery lay to the north of it, not far from Stratford-upon-Avon and the great Warwick Castle.

The way led mostly through farming country, with here and there a small town, its houses clustering close together, with steep, lichen-covered roofs. They passed rolling downs where cattle grazed tranquilly. Fellow travelers were few, but now and then they passed an old man at sundown driving home the sheep, occasionally some miscreant sitting in the stocks, a group of hunters, muskets poised for deer; tall yew hedges, water-mills, farm carts creaking along lazily on narrow, rutted lanes. Every town, every vista, brought scenes of serenity. Most of the country people made respectful way for the travelers, but here and there they were regarded sullenly, and the Marquess was amazed at the number of Roundheads.

This seemed not to bother George. Whenever they stopped at an inn he was sure to flirt with the serving maids, who giggled and smirked at him, elated at his attention.

"How can you?" asked his sister when they had taken to the road again. "How can you make so free with people of that sort? Oh, one must treat them kindly, of course," she added, repeating what she had been taught. "One must be courteous to them, but it's never wise to go beyond that with serving people. I couldn't. I couldn't ever be really friendly with anyone beneath me."

George smiled. "You sound just like Mother. And yet we depend upon these people. Think! Whatever would we have done without Cheam?"

"Cheam knows her place," answered Hal.

Dear Mrs. Cheam! How nice it would be to see her again! Mrs. Cheam, she figured, must be in her late fifties now, but you would never think it to look at her, for her face was unlined and she moved with the agility of a young girl.

When Hal and George were little, Nancy Cheam had been their nurse, a quiet, calm, trustworthy woman who had since been promoted to the post of housekeeper at Langdon Hall. When you thought of Mrs. Cheam you thought of wisdom, of efficiency, serenity and kindliness.

George's mention of Mrs. Cheam brought back the memory of Jerry Vane. The boy's parents having died of the plague when he was six, his grandmother, Mrs. Cheam, had assumed charge of him.

Hal vividly recalled the day she had first seen him, a scrawny, sun-browned, wiry lad—barefooted, shabby and lonely, with a wide and loveable grin. She was four and George was six, and living on that enormous estate they had no playmates. With a total lack of class consciousness they had welcomed Jerry Vane, and during play times the three were always together. Hal had been filled with admiration for this boy who could do everything better than herself and her brother. He could roll a hoop faster, leap higher, climb trees with the swiftness of a monkey, ride like a centaur, use the tallest stilts. At lesson times she was always impatient to have the session over with so she could go outside and join Jerry. Jerry was her hero, her champion, her ever-delightful friend.

Presently Jerry was sharing the lesson times with them, and though now she and George labored to excel him, he invariably knew all the answers. He was permitted to join their studies because of the goodheartedness of Edward Wade.

One day when his children were with their tutor studying near one of the windows in the great hall, the Marquess had chanced to discover Mrs. Cheam's grandson as close as he could possibly get to the window and listening avidly. For a time Edward Wade had watched, amused at the intensity of the little fellow. His own children endured, rather than enjoyed, their hours of schooling, but this boy was oblivious to everything but the lessons! Finally the master of Langdon had spoken to the lad.

"What are you doing, listening at that window?"

The boy had turned to him, startled. Expecting a scolding, he had started to run away.

"Here! Come back!" called the Marquess.

Obediently, Jerry approached him. "Yes, sir. Excuse me, sir. I wasn't doing any harm. I didn't think you'd mind if I just listened."

"How often do you listen?"

"Oh, every day, sir, if it isn't raining. Oh, sir, I want to learn! I want to so very much! You won't forbid it, sir? Please, sir?"

"Forbid it? Odds fish, why should I? In fact, another student will cost me nothing. You don't have to hide. Come every day and take your schooling properly if it's so important to you."

"Oh, sir, thank you—thank you!"

After that at class times Jerry would appear in his Sunday suit, wearing shoes, his black hair neatly combed, his eyes shining. He was amazingly apt, learning quickly and eagerly, drinking it all in as though actually athirst for knowledge. The tutor had to admit to the Marchioness that the Vane boy was a far better student than her own offspring.

Lessons over, Jerry would dash back to his grandmother's cottage, to emerge a few minutes later barefooted and in his old clothes. What fun they had, the three of them, playing hoodman blind, riding races over the fields, screaming with

31

sheer exuberance. It went on like that until Hal was ten, and one day Hal entered her mother's room to find Mrs. Cheam standing before the Marchioness, her eyes grave.

"I understand perfectly, madam," she was saying mildly. "I didn't realize they were nearly grown up. I'll see that it is stopped immediately."

"See that what's stopped?" asked Hal after the older woman had left.

"Come close to me, Hal. You are getting to be a young lady now. I want to explain something to you. You and George are not to play with Jerry any more. Not that he isn't a fine boy, but——"

"Not play with Jerry?"

"It is time for you to understand that one must find his friends among his own class. Some people are born to serve and others to be served. The two cannot mix. One group is superior, the other is inferior. One must give commands, the other must obey them. That is the way the world is."

There followed a long, earnest explanation, gently but firmly given, about the unsurpassable gulf between "quality" and commoners. It seemed there were people who were born to high estate. Others were of coarser mold. Those who were meant to serve must never presume to be on equal terms with those who were served. Henceforth Hal must continue to be pleasant to Jerry, to be considerate and courteous, but she must no longer think of him as her friend.

Infinitely depressed, aware of a deep sense of loss, Hal returned to her own room and sobbed for a long time. She wept because she must cease to associate with one so jolly, so agreeable, so brave and so good. She wept because of the established rules, because she had lost one whom she loved as much as her brother, because of that cruel, unbridge-

32

able gulf, because Jerry was one of "the common people."

Evidently his grandmother lost no time in explaining this to him.

Henceforth he was to "know his place and stay in the position God had put him in." He was lowly. Lady Henrietta and Lord George were "gentry." Nothing could change that. Besides, now that he was twelve it was time he earned his keep.

Jerry ceased to attend the classes and he never showed up for play. You would find him in the stables assisting the grooms, dirty and disheveled, shoveling manure, watering the horses, sweeping out the stalls. When Hal approached, he kept his eyes on the ground, touched his cap and replied in monosyllables.

The Marquess agreed with his wife. She had acted wisely. But the boy was so eager for learning—it was a pity to deprive the lad of that. He spoke to Mrs. Cheam about it, offering to send the boy to Cambridge where he would have the tutoring he so sorely desired and where in time he could enter college. Mrs. Cheam was touchingly grateful. The Marchioness equipped Jerry with the clothes George no longer wore. Mrs. Cheam altered them and a little later Jerry left Langdon Hall. Hal had not seen him since.

"By the way," she asked out of a prolonged silence, "your mention of Cheam made me remember Jerry Vane. Is he still at Cambridge, Father?"

"Yes, and doing brilliantly. I'm proud of the boy. I often get letters from his teachers commending him."

"I wonder if he has become a Puritan?" mused George. "I hear Cambridge is a hotbed for that breed."

"Jerry? A Puritan?" asked Hal in a shocked voice. "No, never! He's much too sensible."

"I don't know about that," replied her father, "but one

33

of his teachers is John Milton, the poet, and Milton certainly has leanings in that direction. He has actually taken the boy into his home as some sort of assistant. Jerry's last letter said I need send no more money, for he was now able to pay his own keep. I had a letter from Milton, too. It declared that Jeremiah Vane was one of the finest young men he had ever met, and an outstanding student."

"I can't imagine Jerry's ever becoming a Puritan," answered Hal. "He was always so full of fun."

What did it matter to her what Jerry had become? Let him be a Puritan. It was no concern of hers. But as she thought back upon those happy days of her childhood she remembered him with affection. The laughter they had shared, how he had always defended her against George's teasing, how he had always protected her. Jerry must be almost twenty now.

She forgot him when they passed through Shottery, a small, quiet village, humble and tidy, with unpaved, narrow lanes bordered by strips of one- and two-story half-timbered houses with dormer windows and thatched roofs; women with long aprons over homespun gowns; boys and old men fishing in the Avon.

Langdon Hall was two miles beyond the village. How proud, how calm, how secure it looked, sitting regally upon its knoll! They turned into a wide driveway overlooked by an entrance tower, and dozens of hounds popped out from behind the holly hedges to bark a tumultuous welcome. Gardeners, feeding the enormous lawn with fall fertilizer, ceased their work to remove their hats as the cavalcade passed.

Hal beamed at them, lifting one hand in greeting. Her world might change; the King's power might be threatened; but Langdon Hall remained—aloof from all that, uninvaded and untouched by conflict and hatred and peril.

Home.

Never had it seemed so beautiful to her.

3 ✿

Christmas

LANGDON HALL WAS A HUGE, SPRAWLING MASS OF STONE
three stories high with wings on either side, mullioned
windows and many tall, thin chimneys. Its broad front
grounds were bordered by skillfully trimmed yews which
were never permitted to reach a height above five and a
half feet.

The main building had been finished during the days of
Henry VII, enlarged in the reign of Henry VIII, and enlarged again in the times of Elizabeth and James. The
servants' wing was off the kitchen in the rear. The stables
were spacious and impressive, and separated from the main
house by about an eighth of a mile. Behind these, entirely
hidden by trees and bushes, was Mrs. Cheam's tidy cottage
—a one-story, whitewashed structure with its own flower
and vegetable gardens which, despite her many duties in
the main house, Nancy Cheam managed to keep weedless
and thriving.

She could have lived in the main house, and tramping
back and forth that eighth of a mile in inclement weather
was decidedly unpleasant, but nevertheless she clung lov-

ingly to her own simple dwelling with its four small rooms, low-raftered ceilings and its bittersweet vines climbing well over the roof.

As the lord of the manor entered through the tall iron gates, passing the entrance tower, grooms sprang forward to take charge of the horses. There was a chorus of salutations.

"Welcome home, my lords and lady."

"It is good to see you, sir."

Nodding pleasantly to their many servants, the family entered the great hall. Here a lively fire awaited them in the enormous hearth, and the sixty house servants were lined up to curtsy, to bow, to relieve the travelers of their hats, capes and gloves. There was always a special greeting to Mrs. Cheam who, as head of them all, stood in the center, looking, except for a few silver strands in her dark-brown hair, almost the same as when she had cuddled Hal in her arms as a baby. Had Hal been a child, Nancy Cheam would have rushed forward to embrace her, but now she held her place, thin, smiling, dignified, waiting respectfully for Hal to approach her.

"The house has missed you, my lady," she said, after a deep curtsy. "Welcome home, ma'am."

"It's good to be back, Cheam. How are you?"

"Quite well, my lady. And you?"

"Oh, fine. Where's Mother?"

"In her room."

"How is she?"

"Not so good as when you left, my lady, but now that you're all home again, she'll doubtless improve." She curtsied to Edward and George. "Welcome, my lords."

With a good-natured, "How are you, Cheam?" they strode past her and ran up the broad stairs to the room on the second floor where the Marchioness waited in her chair by the fireplace, a large pink coverlet over her useless legs, and wearing a pearl gray dressing gown of soft velvet. Longingly she reached out her arms to them.

"Oh, my dears, at last!"

Hal was shocked at how much her mother had aged in this past year and how thin she had gotten.

"Mother, how are you?" she asked after they had kissed.

"I'm better now that we're all together again. How are things in London, Edward? Sit down, all of you, and give me the court gossip."

Mrs. Cheam, without having been told to do so, sent up refreshment for the travelers, and while they ate, the Marchioness must be told all the news of the court. How fared the Queen and how was she taking this prolonged unpleasantness with Parliament? How were the young princes and princesses? Was it true that Puritanism was growing so rapidly?

"England is becoming more fanatical every day," said her husband. "It's no longer the England we grew up in, Anne. There are sad times ahead."

"For us, Edward?"

"For everyone. It must come."

"You mustn't leave me again, any of you!"

"Oh, but I shall have to return to the Queen," said Hal. "I promised faithfully."

"But not until after Christmas, my dear, not until spring. Stay at least until then. I'm lonely without you and I worry about you, what with all this talk of fighting, and those unruly, disgusting mobs in London."

"Doesn't Cheam take good care of you, sweetheart?" asked George.

"Oh, yes. Cheam is wonderful. I don't know what I'd do

38

without her. Promise me, all of you, that if anything should happen to me you'll always take care of her."

"That's understood, my dear," said Edward. "Now you must tell us about yourself. Does the doctor give much encouragement?"

"No. I can only move from this chair to my bed now, and that with difficulty."

Soon after this, when Hal went to her room, she at once wrote an affectionate letter to the Queen, promising to return to court in the spring.

Life at Langdon Hall seemed dull after living for a year at court, especially since their neighbor-castle, Warwick, about ten miles away, was closed because of the absence of its owners. Usually there had been much entertainment between the two great houses, and ordinarily Langdon Hall had many guests, but these days the aristocrats considered it wise to stay at home or at court.

Now and then a minstrel stopped by and when he had enlivened them with his repertoire, moved on. In the evenings the Marchioness was carried downstairs to the great hall where the family got together, Hal playing her lute, and the four pleasant voices blending in song, for singing was one of the favorite pastimes in those pre-war days of Charles Stuart's England.

Daytimes, weather permitting, Hal made charity visits among the sick of the townspeople and the tenants, bringing them food delicacies, some clothing and some money. At other times she and her father and George raced over the fields, their splendid horses taking the hedges with ease.

Too, since her mother was incapacitated, Hal had to assume the duties of lady-of-the-house and visit the various household departments, making sure that all was spic and span—the kitchen, the dairy, the solarium, the scullery and the still room where the herbs were drying.

Her father and brother also had their duties. For miles surrounding the castle the land belonged to the Marquess, who rented it to farmers. These, with the overseer, must be visited and accounts adjusted.

Every Sabbath there was church. Services were conducted by the vicar of Shottery in the Wades' own chapel on the grounds. Though at times Hal missed the activities of the court, she loved her home, loved to stroll about its wide park with its oaks and beeches, its herons and deer herds, its charming fish pond; and she loved to sit quietly reading on the banks of the Avon, for the weather that year was mild, almost springlike.

The first snowstorm came at Christmas. The approach of Christmas brought an increased busyness to the big house, and many mouth-watering odors emanated from the kitchen. The usual celebration was to be held for the tenants, servants and villagers in the main hall, with its beautifully molded plaster ceiling and tall, Italianate fireplace. Here they would toast the King and the royal family, the Marquess and the Marchioness, and receive gifts of money.

In the latticed minstrels' gallery musicians would play for dancing. The hall would be decorated with pine boughs, holly branches and mistletoe. From the walls looked down an impressive array of full-length paintings of bygone Wades as well as past monarchs, including a life-size portrait of Henry VIII with a white feather in his hat and the order of the Garter below his fat, left knee.

The Marquess was a generous man, especially at Christmas. Three huge oak tables spread with white cloths were laden with an abundance of trenchers bearing a fat, succulent goose stuffed with chestnuts; a small roast pig with an apple in its mouth; pigeons browned and juicy; roast duck; capons; a swan; a variety of pastries; plum puddings, hot buns; big bowls of grog, cider and malmsey; dates, apples and cheese.

Everyone came dressed in his best and prepared for a hilarious time, for there were no Puritans in the immediate neighborhood. England might be in trouble, but on that gala Christmas of 1641 there was no evidence of it at Langdon Hall.

Not mixing with the commoners, the Wades sat on a low platform. Occasionally George would bound from it to take some attractive girl around the waist and enjoy several turns about the room with her.

During midafternoon, as Hal was looking on, smiling, she saw Mrs. Cheam enter with a young man wearing a simple doublet made of fustian. His breeches were well-fitting, tubular, but with no lace or fringes at the knees. He was tall, lithe, slim-hipped like an athlete, and his coal-black hair, curling crisply, was closely clipped! His was a lean, strong, clean-shaven face with high cheekbones and white, flashing teeth which he showed in a wide and engaging grin as Mrs. Cheam proudly introduced him to the maids. Hal noted that the unmarried ones boldly flirted with him, their eyes filled with admiration.

"Odds fish," whispered the Marquess, "we've a Roundhead here!"

"It's Jerry," exclaimed Hal. "It's Jerry Vane!"

Then her eyes flashed angrily. How dared Jerry become a Puritan?

He was looking toward them now and George signaled him to approach. At once he left off talking to the pretty girl who seemed determined to hold his attention and made his way through the crowd, finally bowing before the lord and his family. It was not the bow of a courtier, low, practiced and smiling, with a graceful sweep of the right arm. It was the bow of a servant, stiff and somber.

"Glad to see you again, Jerry," said George. "Merry Christmas."

"And a right merry Christmas to you, my lord."

"So, you're back, my boy," said the Marquess genially. "When did you arrive?"

"At noon, sir."

"How long will you stay?"

"Probably until spring, sir."

"Are your studies over, then?"

"Oh, I hope not, sir. I have the honor to be taught by one of the wisest men alive, Mr. John Milton, who took me abroad with him. We returned only recently. I hope soon, sir, to pay you back for all that you have——"

"Nonsense. I want no repayment. Have you turned Puritan, for heaven's sake? If so, what are you doing here? Would you fight your King?"

The young man's eyes turned grave and his pleasant voice was charged with deep feeling. "Sir, I hope never to fight the King or anyone else, but I believe in the principles of Mr. Milton. I believe in liberty."

"Oh?" In Hal's lovely eyes there was more than a hint of sarcasm, "and what are the principles of the omniscient Mr. Milton?"

"This is scarcely the time, my lady, to——"

"Come, tell us!" Her voice was tart and challenging. "We are ignorant here."

"My lady," he replied meekly, "it is Mr. Milton's belief —and mine, too—that the people should have sovereign power through their representatives, that every man should be free as to religion. He says, 'No man who knows right

42

can be so stupid as to deny that all men are naturally free born.' "

"What nonsense!" scoffed the Marquess.

"Oh, really!" exclaimed the Marchioness irately. "Your poor grandmother! She must be heartily ashamed that you have imbibed such fantastic, impractical notions."

"My grandmother, madam, has the intelligence to admit that though she may not share my views I have a right to them."

"Well," said George, injecting a tone of levity into the serious conversation, "if you're a Puritan, Jerry, I'll wager you'll not be among the dancers, and there are several pretty lasses who'll be disappointed."

Jerry smiled, that wide, sudden grin of his. "My lord, I trust I shall never be guilty of disappointing a lady."

"Why," said the Marquee, scowling, "I thought you Roundheads considered dancing and such things sinful."

"Sir, there are Puritans who go to extremes—those who deem laughter a quality of Satan. I'm not among them. Like my teacher, Mr. Milton, I'm a liberal Puritan."

"A liberal Puritan?" asked George. "I didn't know there were any."

Without answering, Jerry let his gaze rest admiringly upon Hal, who was sitting with her head haughtily high. Much to her chagrin, she found herself blushing.

"May I wish your ladyship a merry Christmas?" asked Jerry.

"The same to you," she replied icily.

He bowed again and turned away.

For Hal, after that, Christmas was nothing short of miserable, though she carefully hid her feelings. It was permissible for her brother to join the dancers occasionally, but she had to sit there, isolated, watching Jerry dancing with

43

her maids and bringing them mugs of cider, and several times some of them lured him to beneath a mistletoe where amid much laughter he gallantly kissed them.

"It doesn't matter to me what he does or what he believes or how he behaves," she told herself sternly.

But all the same, this "liberal Puritan" was attractive— far too attractive. Apparently she was totally unaware of him, yet somehow she knew every move he made. The gift of a handsome brooch had arrived that morning from her fiance, who was still in France—an exquisite fleur de lis design fashioned of diamonds and rubies. She kept touching it nervously, as though it was a kind of shield that would protect her from this fascinating commoner.

Grimly she kept insisting that the first thing tomorrow morning she would ask her father to name the day, and then she would go away, far away, to one of the Duke's strongly fortified estates; and that liberal Puritan with his absurdly short hair and singularly engaging grin could go on dancing and kissing forever for all she cared!

What was he, after all, but a mere servant, a member of the lower classes? And he could never hope to be anything else. A man without a penny, whose ancestors had bowed low before "quality." What a disgrace it would be if anyone suspected that she, a maid of honor to England's Queen, was in the least stirred by such a lowly, base-born creature! But what was she thinking of? She wasn't stirred at all. Not a bit. No, not a single, tiny bit.

"I shall plead a headache," she thought, "and get away."

But she didn't. She went on forcing herself to smile, and stayed until the musicians put aside their instruments, until the last "God save you" was said.

"It's been a lovely, lovely Christmas," she announced merrily to her family.

44

"I have a feeling we'll not see another like this," said the Marchioness pensively.

In her room when the candles had been extinguished, Hal lay in her big four-poster bed and sternly forebade herself to cry. Then, angrily, she insisted that she had nothing in the world to cry about.

"What," she wondered, "is the matter with me, anyhow?"

4 ❁

soldiers for the king

NEXT DAY THE WEATHER TURNED STORMY. THE BEECHES cowered before the brutal onslaught of sleet and wind. The servants moved sluggishly, having eaten too much and danced too much the day before. Even George, usually jocular, was in an uncommunicative mood and settled himself in the library by the fire reading a new edition of Shakespeare's works.

Hal found her father in her mother's room, writing letters while his wife worked at her embroidery. Instead of asking him to write the Duke and specify the date of her wedding, Hal found herself saying precisely the opposite.

"Father . . ."

"Yes, my dear?" He glanced up at her after melting the wax of his seal before pressing it to an envelope. "I've written to his Majesty telling him conditions in this part of the country. Well? Well, what is it? You look woeful serious."

"Sir, since that day at Oxford I haven't mentioned the Duke. Now I beseech you, dear Father, if you love me, return this brooch to him and insist that the troth be broken!"

46

Shocked, the Marchioness laid aside her embroidery. "What are you saying! Do you realize what an unpleasant position you're placing your father in? Are you mad to want to give up such an alliance?"

"Mother, please. I just cannot bear the thought of marrying him!"

"Maidenly modesty. I quite understand. I confess I felt the same way about marrying your father. You'll get over it, sweet. Of course you must marry."

"Yes. I know that, but——"

"And his Grace is a most estimable man. He will be good to you. Oh, there are many younger men at court, but tell me, can you think of one more eligible—richer? No, not one. Think of the precedence such a marriage will bring you. Henrietta, Duchess of Thewes! You'll be the envy of——"

"But Mother, the Duke is so—so old, so obese, so dull!"

"One doesn't marry a man for his looks, my dear, nor for his gifts as a conversationalist. Anyhow, the contract has been signed. Your father's honor is at stake. Be sensible!"

"Now, now," said the Marquess soothingly, "it isn't good for you to excite yourself, Anne. Let the matter rest until spring. At that time his Grace will probably return from his tour and if Hal feels as she does now I shall have a talk with him."

"He won't come back until he's sure there's no chance of trouble," Hal replied tartly.

But she did not pursue the subject. The sleet had changed to rain, a chill, wild rain, blown with noisy gusts against the windows, pelting mercilessly on the roof. Restless and depressed, Hal sat opposite her father and began a letter to the Queen, again begging leave to remain at Langdon Hall until spring because of her mother's condition.

47

A few hours later when Mrs. Cheam, accompanied by a maid, brought in her mother's lunch, she wanted to ask about Jerry but decided against it. However, Mrs. Cheam brought up the subject herself.

"I sent for my grandson to come and spend the holidays with me. I haven't seen him for so long, you know. I was sure you wouldn't mind, madam. He can help in the stables, since one of the men is ill with the rheum."

"Of course I don't mind, Cheam. He has turned out to be a fine-looking young man. I've no doubt you are proud of him."

Mrs. Cheam's blue eyes glowed. "Oh, I am, madam! Not so much because he's handsome but because he's learned. He's all I have in the world, you know."

"But," asked the Marquess, "doesn't it distress you that he's a Puritan?"

"No, my lord, no. To my mind a man must decide such things for himself. My Jerry's a high-principled, sensible boy. I think he'll not go to extremes. He was explaining to me the beliefs of the Puritans, and while I don't agree with them altogether, it seems there's much good in them. What I don't like about them, though, is how they try to force their opinions on others—like, for instance, that the whole world's beset by sin."

"I do not care to discuss that objectionable, ridiculous sect," said the Marchioness frigidly.

"No, madam," replied Mrs. Cheam amicably as she arranged the dishes on the table. "There's pheasant, just as your ladyship likes it, and broiled whelks. Will there be anything else, madam?"

"No, you may go. I'll ring."

"Yes, madam."

When she had gone, the Marchioness, who had declared

48

that she did not "care to discuss that objectionable, ridiculous sect," turned to her husband. "Just what are the Puritan beliefs, Edward?"

"Odds fish, how should I know? Except that they favor a simpler form of worship and they label it a sin to bowl on the Sabbath."

"Why are they becoming so strong, these people?" asked Hal. "If their religion is so austere, why do so many people accept it?"

Her father shrugged. "Bless me, I can't figure that out. Let the fish-nosed fools think as they like and don't try to force their weird, severe beliefs on the rest of us! I think it wouldn't be so bad if they kept quiet, but now they've entered into politics where they prate and rant. A lot of them have gone off to the colonies where already they have thirty-three churches. If only the whole lot of them could be shipped there!"

"Yes," agreed Hal feelingly.

"There's one of them in Parliament, a rat-eyed troublemaker with an extraordinarily long nose, a fellow named Oliver Cromwell. He stands up and preaches to Parliament, to everyone, 'Follow God! Seek the Lord and His face continually!' He has the idea that everything he does is because the Almighty wills it. The King ought to hang the insufferable fellow. Well, Hal, let's not permit the thought of Cromwell to spoil our appetites. Your mother has a good meal, I see. Let's go downstairs and find out what's served to us."

For the next few days the downpour continued and Hal was confined to the house. The routine was unchanged, except that a messenger brought a letter from the Queen, doubtless having passed the Wades' messenger on his way.

The family were in Anne Wade's room, all listening eagerly to Hal as she read it. Her Majesty's letter was long and held a tone of despair. Things were going against the King in Scotland. His Majesty had been compelled to acquiesce to the Scot's demands, agreeing to permit them to adhere to their desired religion.

The Marquess sighed. "If such a privilege has been given to Scotland, then it will have to be given to England and Ireland. It means an open challenge to the Stuart system."

"It's clear to me," said George, "that the King's forces have little will to fight. Go on, Hal. What else does her Majesty say?"

Hal read that the King had pronounced the Scottish uprising to be treason, while Parliament, backing the Scots, declared that they had risen for freedom and were fighting for the liberty of all Englishmen. But the King was not ready to give up in Scotland. Though filled with consternation, he was yet resolute. His troops were more like a mob than an army. Meanwhile, the treasury was empty and the English merchants had refused to grant him a loan.

Her Majesty ended with a reminder that Lady Hal had promised to return to her and hoped it would be soon. She sent her love to the Marchioness and trusted that her condition had improved.

"Hmm," said the Marquess when Hal laid down the letter. "So the merchants have refused to grant him a loan! What disloyalty! Well, it behooves me to aid him all I can. Though what I can give will not go far when it comes to carrying on a war, still it will help. I consider it a matter of duty."

"But Father," asked Hal, "how do you propose to aid the King?"

"This is a time when we must all make sacrifices," announced the Marquess, standing before his family with his plump, white-stockinged legs apart. He was calm and he was decisive. "I shall take all our plate, all our pewter, all my personal jewels and as much money as I can spare, and deliver them to his Majesty!"

"All our plate?" asked Hal. "That would mean we shall have to eat on wooden trenchers!"

"All our plate, in itself, would make a goodly load," said George.

"Did—did you say, Edward," the voice of the Marchioness faltered pathetically, "that you would deliver it to his Majesty yourself? You mean you're going to join his forces?"

"My dear, I'm only doing what every loyal Englishman ought to do. It's my duty to fight for the King."

"Let me go in your stead, Father," begged George.

"Yes, Edward," said the Marchioness, her thin, colorless lips twitching nervously, "George is younger."

"Besides," put in George cheerily, "it will be an exciting adventure. Yes, I'll go, Father."

"Very well, my boy. Come, Anne, no tears. I'm sure this trouble will end speedily, perhaps even by spring, if the King can get enough arms and money. Well, let us begin the collection at once. Ring for the servants, Hal. We'll need barrels."

When she had pulled the bell cord, Hal stripped off the rings she wore, the necklace, earrings and the magnificent brooch her fiance had sent from France. "Take these."

"Bring me my jewel casket," ordered the Marchioness, and began to cry.

"Now, now, my dear," said the Marquess with a soothing pat on her shoulder, "if it hurts you to part with them——"

"Part with them?" she asked tearfully. "What are they compared with parting from my only son?"

Hal, too, felt like crying at the thought of parting from

51

George, but her gloom was relieved by the activity which now began and which continued for the next week. She, George and their father went from room to room collecting heavy silver candlesticks, cups, platters, spoons, gold vases, snuff boxes, even gold toothpicks. As to jewels, George and Edward gave all they had, while Hal and her mother gave only the ones they liked least. When the large wagon was packed, Edward went down into the vault, entering it by a secret door known to no one but him and his family, and returned with five large bags of money.

The weather, though cold, was bright and dry on the day that George kissed his mother and sister good-by. Another letter had arrived from one of Edward's friends at court. The King was now at Whitehall in London and resolved upon war.

Since Princess Mary, now ten, had been affianced to the son of the ruling prince of Holland, the Queen was leaving for that country, ostensibly to see her daughter settled on her new home, but her real purpose in going was to raise money for her husband's cause.

England was now being flooded with Puritan pamphlets. Wherever several people gathered there were sure to be political arguments. London was strongly pro-Parliament. The trouble in Ireland had broken out again.

When the final moment of parting came, the Marchioness and her daughter broke into tears, and the Marquess warned his son that he was to avoid all arguments on the journey and make haste to the King. Sadly the family watched George ride off with sixty men-at-arms, all of them, like their young master, ready to sacrifice their lives for the King.

To Hal the world seemed a dismal place that January

after her brother had left. Civil war had now become a certainty. Her brother would be part of it. She missed him sorely and her nerves demanded strenuous action. She went through her closets, discarding many gowns, but this had no soothing effect, so she decided to go for a long ride. Usually she would have sent word to have her favorite horse brought to the front entrance, but today she walked to the stables.

She had not seen Jerry since Christmas and was not even sure that he had not returned to Cambridge, but as she approached the stables she saw him lifting pitchforks of hay into the stalls. Coming closer, she saw that his thick-soled shoes were caked with mud and his hands were dirty. Despite the cold, he wore no hat and his coarsely spun shirt was open at the throat.

"Oh, but he's strong!" she thought; then a moment later she shuddered. "Ugh! Look at his shoes! How can he bear to get dirty like that? Simply repulsive!"

Seeing her now, he stopped his work, leaned the pitchfork against the wall and touched his head respectfully, flashing that wide and magnetic grin.

"Good day to you, my lady."

"Good day," she replied icily. "Please saddle Rosamonde for me."

"At once, your ladyship." He entered the stable and she followed him, lifting her long skirt daintily, and sat on a bench watching him. There was a lengthy pause. "I expect you're lonesome without your brother, ma'am," he said at last.

"Yes."

"I'll be leaving, too, tomorrow."

"Oh?" Her face was impassive. "Back to Cambridge?"

"Yes, my lady."

"If there's war—and there surely will be—I suppose you'll join the Roundheads?"

"And would you expect me to join the Cavaliers?"

"It's quite indifferent to me which side you're on. But you Roundheads are to blame for this trouble."

"Are we now? It would seem to me that the blame should rest on the King." He refused to be put on the defensive. His pleasant voice remained calm. "It seems to me that liberty's a thing worth fighting for, and you'll have to agree that the King has forced us to it. If he'd compromise a bit —just a little——"

She glared at him. "Oh, why don't you go to America with the other Puritans? I wish every one of you would get out of England. Then maybe we'd have peace!"

He remained maddeningly poised. "I've thought of going there, my lady, and since my going would pleasure you, then I might sail sometime; but not now. I've a certain duty to my grandmother, who has the silly notion of not wanting me to go so far away."

"You needn't worry about her. We will always take care of her. So there's nothing, positively nothing, to hold you here. England would be better off with one Puritan the less!"

He turned toward her, grimy hands on his hips, looking straight into her eyes. "I'm sorry that your ladyship is so displeased with me," he replied in a low, even voice.

She found his poise and his good nature irritating, and felt herself to be at a disadvantage. "Why must you labor in the stables?" she asked hotly. "Why must you get yourself so dirty? I'm sure my father hasn't ordered you to do this work."

"No, he hasn't, but I like to earn my keep. I'm beholden

enough to your father as it is, but someday I shall pay him back. I've kept strict account of the money he has put out for me. Besides, where's the disgrace in honest work? When a man does a job, even if it's cleaning the stables, he has a right to know pride in it. I like to work. I was born to it. But I know how you feel. Anyone who works with his hands is lowly, no gentleman, practically scum—far, far beneath you."

"And anyone who fights against his King is a traitor!" she retorted.

Still he remained self-possessed, polite. "My lady, a man fights not so much against something as for something. I am ready to fight for freedom of worship, for the rule of the people through their representatives, such as Parliament. I believe the old way must go, the way in which one man, one alone, wields power."

"I have no interest in what you believe. Please hurry with the saddling."

"Why is my lady in such a hurry?" His voice was soft, his eyes boldly approving. "If I may say so, it's a pleasure, just looking at you."

"You are insolent and presumptuous!"

"So I am, my lady. I apologize for forgetting my place. But a man enjoys looking at whatever he finds pleasing—a sunset, a tree, a shaded stream, a beautiful, beautiful girl."

She blushed, glad that he found her beautiful and annoyed with herself for being glad.

"I didn't come here to be stared at," she said haughtily.

"I know. Well, I'm off tomorrow, so you'll be spared that unpleasantness."

Her heart said, "Must you go? Stay here!" But her voice spoke coldly. "I wish you a happy journey back to Cambridge and I hope you stay there forever!"

He had his back to her and he seemed not to have heard. "Is it true that you're betrothed to the Duke of Thewes?"

"It's true, yes. His Grace is at present sojourning in France. We expect his return probably this summer. At that time our marriage date will be announced."

"What kind of a man is he that would voluntarily go so far away from the one he loves?"

There was no need for her to answer, for he led the horse to her and helped her to mount. She put one leg over the saddle horn and artfully arranged her long velvet skirt. When at last her eyes looked down at him, they grew suddenly gentle.

"Good-by, Jerry."

"Good-by, my lady. God guard you."

He stood watching as she dashed down the driveway. She rode fast that day, too fast, as though she were trying to escape from something, and when she returned she left the horse at the front entrance, letting one of the grooms return it to the stables.

In her own sitting room she flung her plumed hat on a sofa, tore off her richly gauntleted gloves, and asked herself, "What's the matter with me?" There seemed no answer. "What's the matter with me?" she asked again, staring at the wall. Then, because she dared not give an honest explanation, she decided, "It's just because I'm worried about George, about England, about Mother, about the Queen going off to Holland without me, about—oh, about everything!"

Dinner that evening was served in her mother's sitting room close to the fire. The three of them were silent because they missed George and because they were eating from wooden plates.

"Father," Hal began out of a long stillness, "I promised

the Queen I'd return to her as soon as I could. There's really nothing to keep me here."

"Her Majesty is in Holland," he replied gravely.

"I know, but I could be of use to her there."

"You are of use to me here," said the Marchioness. "Your brother has gone. We may never see him again. Your father was saying that he feels it his duty to join the King's forces, too. Could I stand to see you go, also? My plate, most of my jewels, my only son, my husband—and my daughter, too? Must I give up so much to the throne?" Her eyes filled with tears.

Hal patted her hand. "There, Mother. I'll stay. Don't cry. I'll stay."

"That's my girl," said the Marquess approvingly.

February and March passed uneventfully. At the end of April word came from George that he was well and that with the King's forces he had gone to Hull, where there was a large store of arms, but the man who was in charge of them, Sir John Hotham, had refused to open the gates to the King!

The letter went on to say that his Majesty was well and confident and had made him his aide-de-camp.

When next they heard from him it was May. He was with the King's forces at York. They had had no real battle as yet, but Charles, more than ever determined upon war, was still badly in need of funds. His nephew, Prince Rupert, had joined him. A militia was being quickly enrolled and their old neighbor, Lord Warwick, had been given command of the fleet. Women in York were in sympathy with the Royalists and had made what donations they could, even giving up their wedding rings. "If I granted Parliament's demands," Charles had said, "I should be no more than a phantom of a king!"

57

"I feel like a coward, sitting safely and snugly at home," exclaimed the Marquess, putting the letter down and rising to pace the floor. "What am I, an old woman? I must go, Anne! I must!"

She sighed. "I know. I know how you feel. Well, I won't try to hold you here any longer. Your duty is to the King. God help that man!"

"Thank you, my dear, for letting me go. But have no fear. The war will be over in a twinkling. Surely before next Christmas. Meanwhile, you are in good hands with Hal and Cheam."

"Will you have to take more of our men-at-arms, Edward? Surely we'll need them here to guard us."

"I shall take them all. No, don't look so frightened. The Roundheads won't come here. What would they want in Stratford or Shottery? And the King needs all the men he can get. Besides, as sure as I live, this whole thing will be over in a few months."

He seemed young and forceful as he assembled his men and told them to prepare for a march. Not content with that, he went into Shottery, Stratford, Compton, Warwick, Banbury, Honeybourne, Malvern Wells, Great Malvern, Evesham—all the surrounding towns—making speeches, recruiting every able-bodied man he could.

Two weeks later, followed by a hundred of his own retainers, plus a thousand farmers and townsmen and about seventy women who decided to go along and care for their men, the lord of Langdon Hall started for York. In addition to his small army he was taking almost all the money in the vault.

The place was now left unguarded. It was shorthanded, too, since many of the maids had left to join their men. There were only ten elderly men left to care for the extensive grounds and two to manage the stables.

"So few to guard us, Father!" said Hal, as they parted.

"It won't be for long, sweetheart," he said, kissing her. "You'll see, by fall we'll be back. I've left only three horses in the stables and I'm taking a great deal of money, but don't worry, child. You know how to get into the vault and there's enough remaining to take care of your needs until I return. Stay with your mother and watch over her. She's more prone to tears now than she used to be. I suppose that's a phase of her illness. Be patient with her—and pray for us!" He mounted his horse, took off his hat and held it in the air, giving the two rallying cries used by the cavaliers. "Have at you for the King!" and "For God and Queen Mary!"

She watched him go, proud of his patriotism and sharing his assurance that he would, indeed, return before Christmas.

In two weeks the broad lawns were no longer smooth and tidy. Weeds grew in the driveway and the gardens. The house seemed strangely empty. No minstrels came to divert its remaining residents. Mrs. Cheam gave no hint of fear. She shut off all rooms not in use, and remained her cheery, competent self.

"Jerry managed to send me a letter," she said one evening in late May. "I got it this morning. He said Parliament has broken off all negotiations with the King and is energetically preparing for war."

Hal did not look up from her embroidery. "Oh?" she said mildly.

"He said there had been a large parade in London, several thousand civilians carrying placards with one word printed on them—liberty."

"He—he's well?"

"Quite. Thank God the lad has marvelous health. He hasn't yet enlisted because he wants to finish this term at college and he also wants to finish some transcribing work for Mr. Milton."

"The King will win! He must!"

"Oh, indeed, my lady."

"There were mobs and parades in London last year, too. All they did was shout."

"God save the King," answered Mrs. Cheam, as she continued her usual spring chore—strewing herbs in every room "to sweeten the house." From a large basket she took handfuls of balm, basil, lavender, red mint, cowslips and sweetbrier. "But Parliament holds London, you know," she added significantly. "If the King wins, it looks as though he's going to have a long, hard fight for it."

Hal did not answer.

5 ✿

tragedy

THE WEEK FOLLOWING THE DEPARTURE OF THE MARQUESS,
his wife took a decided turn for the worse. For two months
Hal rarely left her. Night and day she was in attendance,
watching that life drift painlessly away. During that ag-
onizing time she often asked herself how she could have
stood it without Mrs. Cheam. Their positions were re-
versed now. Class distinctions no longer existed. It was
Mrs. Cheam who gave the orders.

"Your ladyship must go to bed and get some rest. . . .
My lady, you must eat. . . ." and drugged with anguish,
Hal obeyed. Mrs. Cheam's hand was always there in the
long, dismal night hours, soothing, comforting. Mrs.
Cheam's voice, low and loving, brought the solace she
needed. "You must never believe for one moment that
death is the end, my lady. . . . No, now, don't be ashamed
to cry. . . ."

Then, at three o'clock one morning in early July, it
was over. Like a small child, Hal turned from the bed and
moved into Mrs. Cheam's strong, consoling arms and felt
herself encompassed by love. Both women were exhausted

from their long, heartrending vigil. There was no way to get word to Edward and George, for Hal did not know where the King's forces were; besides, it was necessary that the deceased be buried quickly.

Tired as she was, it was Mrs. Cheam who took charge of everything—saw to the preparing of the funeral feast, the measuring of the coffin, the washing and robing of the corpse; ordered the digging of the grave in the chapel, the mourning garments for Hal and the servants, the tolling of the bell.

Even now the ordeal was not over. As chief mourner, Hal was required to hold a night-long wake. In a small, bare room off the chapel she must sit with the casket during the seemingly interminable nocturnal hours, while tall candles at the head and foot of the coffin emphasized the spectral hush. She must sit there, robed in dull black; but she was not alone. Nancy Cheam, also in black, was beside her. Her shoulder was there to weep on and her hand covered Hal's in tenderness and wordless sympathy.

And during the dreadful, seemingly endless vigil a change took place in Henrietta Wade. Through the sharpness and pain of her grief her pride in birth and position melted into nothingness, and she saw clearly how foolish and how conceited she had been.

"How dared I think," she mused within that sacred silence of death and sorrow, "that a mere accident of birth made me superior to her? What a fool I've been, what a snob! She is better than I—far better, wiser, stronger. God forgive me for my arrogance! God help me never to make this mistake again. Don't let me look down on anyone merely because my father is richer and has a title! Oh, dear God, thank you—thank you for my darling Cheam!"

When at last the sun rose, Mrs. Cheam left to bring

in some men who were to carry the coffin into the chapel. The minister arrived, with a lengthy oration written on long sheets of paper. Then silently, gravely, with downcast heads, the few remaining servants, the tenants, the villagers came, filling the chapel. Though always aloof from them, the Marchioness had been kind. Silently, sorrowfully, they placed their flowers, freshly picked from their gardens, beside the coffin. The minister droned on, expanding his lengthy eulogy, his voice rising and falling dramatically. Then came his prayers, equally long-winded and tedious, and Hal thought that she must surely faint.

But finally it was over. The coffin was lowered and a flat stone placed above it. The people walked slowly to the castle where a feast had been prepared for them.

"It's into bed with you, my lady," said Mrs. Cheam as she and Hal entered the side door. "I'll send up some food. You're burdened with grief and weary with this long vigil. You're to stay abed for the next two days!"

Eyelids swollen with weeping, Hal nodded dully, like a person who had been drugged. Not now did she resent being ordered about. She was humbly grateful for it.

"Cheam," she murmured brokenly, "how can I thank you? What can I say——?"

"Say nothing. Though to others you're a grown-up young lady, to me you're still a little girl. When you were a child and you'd hurt yourself, whose arms did you run to but mine? And now you're hurt worse than you've ever been— maybe worse than you'll ever be again—and I can't do anything to help. I can only love you and take care of you. Go to your room now and try to get some sleep. I'll be up as soon as I can with a cumin poultice for your poor eyes."

"But you, too, need rest. I'd rather that you got into bed and let me serve you."

63

"No argument," replied Mrs. Cheam firmly. "For once you'll do as you're told. Upstairs now, and close the door so none of the chatter can reach you."

Hal's maid helped her to undress and was then dismissed. Yes, it was good to get in bed, but there the realization of her aloneness engulfed her and she sobbed. Alone. Perhaps at this very moment her father and brother were facing death; perhaps even now one or both of them were suffering. And Jerry? Where was he? Suddenly Jerry seemed as much a part of her family as George. She remembered how rude she had been at their last meeting and said to herself that he had every right to hate her.

Tired as she was, sleep seemed impossible. Now that her mother was gone there was nothing to do but go to Holland and Queen Mary. There was nothing to hold her to Langdon Hall now, except that she disliked the thought of leaving Mrs. Cheam. Her sobs ceased, but the knowledge of her aloneness was frightening. True, she was fond of the Queen, who had obviously grown to trust and depend upon her, and she had been happy at court, being close to her Majesty, being admired and flattered by Cavaliers who, knowing of her betrothal to the powerful Duke of Thewes, had been always discreet in their attentions. But somehow, being admired and catered to no longer seemed as attractive as it had once been.

She managed a smile as Mrs. Cheam, followed by two black-robed maids, entered the room carrying trays which they placed on a table near the bed; and then, at a gesture from the housekeeper, the women quietly left the room.

Mrs. Cheam had reverted to her role of servant. "Will your ladyship remain at Langdon Hall?" she asked.

"No. I was thinking there's nothing to keep me here now. The Queen is in Holland. I shall rest a few weeks and then join her."

"Pardon, my lady, if I may say so, I'm not sure that that's wise. These are not good days to go a-traveling. There are pockets of Roundheads prowling about. They have no love for aristocrats, but you'd be a special target for their animosity."

"I? How so? I've never harmed them."

"Everybody knows that Lady Henrietta Wade is especially close to the Queen—and the Queen, even more than the King—is held responsible for this mess. To harm you would actually be, in their minds, like harming her. Jerry warned me of this before he left. He said that if any Parliamentary forces should come I was to hide you and swear you were not here. All sorts of people are joining the Parliamentary forces, you know, not just Puritans. Some of them are nothing but rowdies from the slums of London. Besides, if you were to leave here, what sort of escort could you have? There are only twelve elderly men on the grounds and three horses in the stable. That would mean you'd have only two men to guard you. That's not enough, my lady. As things are, for you to make that journey would be dangerous, very."

"I see. Yes, you're right; still, I promised the Queen I'd come to her. I know she was devoted to my mother and I believe she's fond of me. I'm honored in having her complete confidence. She has told me things she wouldn't tell to anyone else save the King."

"A hot-tempered, imperious woman, I hear, but with considerable charm. They say it's she who has goaded the King into taking this stand. The people will never forgive her for that. If Parliament could get its hands on her—my, she'd be arrested so quick!"

"Still, I must go to her. It's my duty. I promised."

"Well, I can't stop you if you feel that you must go, but you'd better go disguised."

"Disguised? I hadn't thought of that. As what?"

"As a boy. Yes, that would be better. As a middle-class boy. Dressed like that it would be easier to hide if you had to, easier than wearing these long, full skirts. Besides, you wouldn't attract so much attention. A girl as beautiful as you would always attract attention, be she garbed in satin or linsey-woolsey."

"Dressed as a boy! But then I'd have to cut my hair to my shoulders. Oh, I couldn't! I—I've always been proud of my hair."

"It would grow again. It is one more sacrifice to make for the throne. Reconcile yourself to it, my lady. Now then, traveling that far you'd certainly need some money. How much of that do you have, if you'll excuse me for making so bold?"

"I don't know how much Father left in the vault. Besides, the servants' wages are due this month and I wouldn't dream of going off without paying them. But I know Father gave most of it to the King. Of course, I still have my jewels and there are a few left of Mother's."

"I shall start making you a boy's wardrobe, and I've some of Jerry's clothes that he has long since grown out of."

"Is Jerry—have you heard from him? Is he all right?"

"As far as I know. The minister told me there was a man at the inn, a Roundhead who was bound for Cambridge, probably one of Parliament's spies. I asked no questions, but I wrote a letter to Jerry, sending it in care of Mr. John Milton, and I asked the minister to give it to this man. I told Jerry how things were here—the lack of guards and all —and I said we needed him. I doubt that he'll get the letter. For all I know he's in the army, off heaven knows where."

66

"Is there any news from the army—either army? These last few weeks I've quite forgotten that there's a war. If only I knew that Father and George were safe!"

"I heard that Parliament was raising a large force. And the name they give it! 'For defense of the King and the Parliament.' Defense of the King, indeed! Just let them get their hands on him! Yet they don't want to kill him—not really. Such an idea is abhorrent. They only want to compel him to relinquish his power. The Earl of Essex is the Captain-General and the Earl of Bedford has been named as its General of the Horse."

"I know them both. How sad that men like that should be fighting against their King! What a queer, topsy-turvy world this is! Do you know how large a force Parliament has?"

"I heard it was twenty thousand foot and four thousand horse soldiers plus the English and Scotch officers that have been drawn from the low countries. They believe that the whole matter will be settled by one battle."

"Why should they think so?"

"Because they know the King is practically destitute of arms and funds. He's trying desperately to raise recruits, but the people are reluctant. Well now, you settle back and try to get some sleep. I'll give orders not to disturb you."

During the next week the inevitable reaction from Hal's ordeal took its toll. Drained of energy, her sorrow mounting in that merciless, persistent way that sorrow has, she remained close to the house. Realizing the danger of the trip she proposed to make, she was undecided whether to leave or not; besides, she could not rid herself of this strange, aching sense of physical weakness.

It was the natural result of prolonged strain, tension and anxiety, but she was so unaccustomed to the feeling of

67

debility that she began to wonder whether she was actually ill and if, having begun the journey, she would be able to complete it.

Thinner and pale, she sometimes went for long walks to the Avon or up to the knoll where the beeches were. Below her in a distance she could see Shottery with its modest plaster and timber cottages, thatched roofs and narrow, curving lanes. From this vantage point the sunsets were magnificent. It was an inspiring view, revealing a calm little world that was untouched by conflict, a tidy oasis in the midst of struggle, quaint and content.

She rarely met anyone on these solitary strolls, but once she encountered a trio of boys who were going fishing in the river. At sight of the elegant, black-clad figure they swiftly removed their hats and stepped aside for her to pass.

She smiled at them and they smiled back, eager to please the lady of Langdon Hall.

"Have you heard how the war is going?" she asked.

"Yes, my lady. They say Parliament holds London and the King holds Oxford. They say Parliament wants to capture Oxford and the Royalists want to take London. Some Roundheads came through Stratford and Great Malvern and Shottery trying to get men to enlist. They said the King can't win. They wanted to know who was living at Langdon Hall now and how many men-at-arms were there."

"Why would they want to know that?"

The boys shook their heads, not answering.

"Well, thank you," said Hal. "Good fishing."

She returned to the house, not wanting to meet anyone else. After reaching it, she was at a loss for something to do. Embroidery? No, she was too restless. She wandered into the library, fingering books by Marlowe, Shakespeare, Chaucer, Spenser and Sidney, but she was in no mood for reading. Next, she picked up her lute, strummed a few chords and put it aside.

Then she went into the garden and picked a bouquet of carnations, gillyflowers and roses, and carried them in a small urn to her mother's grave. It was cool and restful in the chapel and she sat there, not praying but trying to face the future. And what did her future hold, anyhow? Being married to a man of wealth and importance, a man she did not love. She preferred not to think about him. Soon she must start off in quest of the Queen—yes, even without an escort, as soon as she felt strong enough, she must go.

The thought of leaving Langdon Hall brought an increased sense of sadness. But she had to go—because she had promised, because the motto of her family had always been "Duty and Loyalty." She read the words now on a stained glass window, below the Wade coat of arms.

The trip to the seacoast would be long. She did not know how long, but she reckoned it would take at least a week or maybe two. Then it meant finding a ship to Holland, for surely if the Queen had left there she would have known it. A letter would have come or someone in the village would have heard it from a traveler, for news like that would be difficult to keep secret. Cheam was wise in advising her to travel as a boy, but she shrank from the thought of cutting her hair, which reached to well below her waist.

Finally, after a lengthy prayer, she left the chapel, still weary and depressed, and made her way back through a cobbled path that led to the landscaped garden. Wide stone steps led from a terrace to a large, round fish pond where there were several stone benches beneath spreading oaks.

Walking down the steps, she seated herself on one of the benches, conscious of the singular lethargy that had possessed her since the death of her mother.

The lethargy dissipated magically at the sight of a tall, muscular figure coming swiftly toward her. How vital he looked, how charged with life and energy. Oh, but it was good to see him!

Reaching her, he removed his hat and bowed. For the first time his clipped hair was not offensive. Instead, she thought it looked neat and manly.

"At my lady's service," he said respectfully.

"Jerry! Oh, Jerry, I'm glad you're back!"

"I started as soon as I received Grandmother's letter. I arrived quite late last evening."

"You're needed here. I know she misses you greatly. You'll stay now?"

"As long as I can be of use to you, my lady. Grandmother told me you intend to leave soon. You'll surely need an escort."

"Do you think I shall be in any real danger?"

"There's danger everywhere, ma'am. Yesterday I passed about three hundred ruffians. They claimed to be Roundheads and they'd have given me a bad time had they not realized that I was a fellow in the same class as themselves and without money or jewels. They were moving in this direction, but they may not come to Shottery. They said they were bound for Northampton or Nottingham or wherever the King is, hoping to engage his followers in a fight."

"But even if they come this way surely they wouldn't harm me?"

"They have already razed several castles and they boasted of their hatred of all aristocrats. When they learned I was headed for Shottery they mentioned Langdon Hall and how it had been left without adequate defenses and how they had heard that the Queen's closest friend lived here."

"Oh! What—what shall I do, Jerry?"

"Don't be alarmed. They may not come here at all. They are unfamiliar with the district and they might take some other road. But I wish the Marquess had been somewhat less loyal to the King and left a better guard."

"He was convinced that the trouble would be over long before this."

"Over! It hasn't really begun yet."

"That settles it. My going to the Queen, I mean. I shall leave next week. How I shall get to Holland I have no idea. I—I'm frightened, Jerry."

This in itself was an indication of how much she had changed, for she had been brought up never under any circumstances to show fear before a menial. But it was impossible now for her to think of Jerry as a menial. He was her friend and she needed him.

"Aye," he said solemnly, "there's much to fear these days. I advise you, my lady, not to go for any walks outside the grounds and lock your bedroom door at night—at least until we know that those cutthroats have left the vicinity."

"Very well," she promised meekly. "Jerry, how much longer do you think this will last?"

"Until the King gives up."

"He'll die first."

"If only he'd give up! If only he'd compromise! Nobody really wants to kill him. He could live in peace and his country could live in peace except for his mulish determination to be an absolute ruler as the Tudors and his father were. Is the man blind? Can't he realize that the people won't submit to that any more?"

"But they must submit to it. He's a good man, Jerry,

He isn't cruel, immoral and unscrupulous as Henry the VIII was. If he believes in the divine right of kings, this conviction is inbred in him. He couldn't be expected to renounce it. But let's not talk of that any more. It's a subject on which we couldn't be expected to agree. Jerry, how shall I get to Holland?"

"We must make a direct line to the sea—the Straits of Dover."

"We?"

"I shall be with you—naturally," he answered quietly.

She felt like crying, so grateful she was for his loyalty, his concern. For a few moments she sat there, opening and closing her black lace fan, a lovely, graceful figure in black satin and pearls, which made her skin seem petal-like in its fairness.

"Your grandmother said I should go disguised as a boy."

"I agree. We'll start as soon as Grandmother finishes some clothes for you."

"Yes. Oh, Jerry, I'm so glad you'll be with me! I'm sure with you beside me I won't be afraid."

He looked away from her. There was a slight pause, then she rose and started up the broad stairway to the terrace, he moving beside her, hat in hand, eyes on the ground. Reaching the top of the stairs she turned to him, speaking in a low, unsteady voice.

"I—I want you to know how grateful I am for your loyalty."

"My grandmother and I owe much to your family," he replied stiffly, steeling himself against the appealing sadness in her big, clear eyes. "Through the generosity of your father I have been given a fine education. When this trouble is over I shall be able to get a position as a tutor or a secretary. Perhaps someday I shall be a member of Parliament. You think I'm boasting? Well, at least I can try."

They continued their walk across the terrace. At the door to the house she turned and faced him.

"Thank you for everything, Jerry. I apologize for being so rude the last time we met."

His eyes were soft, unguarded, tender, and he seemed not to have heard, so entranced was he by her beauty.

"Grace was in her steps, heav'n in her eye,
In every gesture dignity and love."

She smiled. "Are you quoting from some poem?"

"Pardon, your ladyship. I just happened to recall one of Mr. Milton's verses."

"I have never read them. Is he a great poet?"

"Yes. Someday I would like to read some of his work to you."

"Quote something else from his writings."

"Let me see now. Oh, yes, here's one. 'Who kills a man kills a reasonable creature, God's image; but who destroys a good book kills reason itself.' "

"I like that. What a pity so wise a man and such an excellent poet should be a Puritan!"

" 'A good book,' he says, 'is the life-blood of a master spirit.' God willing, I shall write a good book one day. Not that I could ever hope to be as great as Mr. Milton, of course."

"I'm sure you'll do quite as well. You probably overrate the man, admiring him so much. Perhaps one day people will be quoting excerpts from the work of Jeremiah Vane." She smiled. "Well, good-by, Jerry. Tomorrow bring me some of Mr. Milton's poems."

"Gladly, my lady."

She entered the house and he turned away, moving lightly down the steps.

Hal was no longer tired, but she felt inexpressibly lonely as she took her evening meal at the long table in the great hall, a table built to accommodate a hundred guests. She wished she could invite Jerry to dine with her, but that, she knew, would cause gossip among the servants.

In her room she asked herself what she should wear tomorrow, for suddenly she wanted to look even more beautiful. It had been over a month since she had cared about what she wore. Tomorrow she would send to Stratford to find out if the bookseller had any books by one John Milton.

"Is her ladyship ready to be undressed now?" asked her maid, entering to find Hal standing dreamily by the window.

"I suppose you're eager to see me safely abed. There's a moon tonight. Ah, what a gorgeous moon! You're wanting to take a stroll with someone, eh?"

"I'll not deny it, m'lady."

"Well, you may turn back the covers and put out my nightshift. I'll undress myself when I'm ready."

"Oh, thank you, m'lady. Very good of you, m'lady."

The maid lost no time in bringing out Hal's nightshift, dressing gown and slippers, turning back the brocaded coverlet, plumping the pillow.

"Goodnight, m'lady. Pleasant dreams."

"Goodnight, Meg. Pleasant strolling."

Though not sleepy, Hal began slowly to undress. Finally in her nightshift—a long, white satin garment edged with lace—she stood at the window again, gazing out at the huge greenwood trees with their wide-spreading branches, their leaves silvered in the moonlight.

Nothing moved out there. The broad lawn looked as if it had been spread with silver frosting by fairy hands. On the farms of her father's tenants the flax had been picked and was drying, the buckwheat had been mowed, the cows led to their stalls. Somewhere in the King's camp her father and brother, if still alive, were probably playing at dice or backgammon with their comrades. And all over England on the quiet lanes youths and maidens were strolling and making love, the silver witchery of the midsummer moon giving them a new eloquence.

Turning away from the window she said her prayers and climbed into bed to stretch out on the thick feather mattresses. The moonlight made large, luminous patches on the floor and she thought how lovely a thing it would be to love and be loved and to walk with one's beloved in the moonlight.

She could think of no one in her circle who had actually married for love, yet most of them seemed happy enough. But there would be no real happiness for her. The Duke was old, with fat hands. Doubtless, had it not been for the war, she would by now be the Duchess of Thewes.

Finally she fell into a disturbed sleep, haunted by the terrifying nightmare that she was in a dank, dark cavern filled with bats and snakes and roaches, and she could not find her way out. Suddenly she was awakened by the frenzied barking of the hounds, the sounds of horses' hoofs and shouts. For a time she imagined that this was part of that horrible dream-experience. Then abruptly she sat up, heart palpitating madly, as she realized that this was real.

Bounding out of bed, she rushed to the window that overlooked the driveway.

The brightness of the moonlight revealed about three hundred riders turning in beneath the entrance tower, not keeping to the driveway but swarming over the wide lawn, converging on the house. They wore no uniforms, but they were armed.

For a moment she wheeled about, dervishlike in panic, not knowing what to do. Then she remembered that, obeying Jerry, she had shot the bolt on her heavy oak door before saying her prayers. She was praying now—wild, gasping prayers—as she shakily lit a candle and feverishly began to dress.

Her hands were trembling so, and her fingers were bungling. Terror-struck, she wondered why women had to wear so many clothes.

"Dear Father—Father in heaven—deliver me from evil! Where're my stockings? Where are my slippers?"

The tumult was increasing, for the men had entered the house. Above the barking, the neighing of horses and the strange voices of the intruders, several maids screamed.

What a long-winded process dressing was! Her corset now, underdrawers, petticoats. Heavy footsteps were racing up the stairs, moving along the corridor, coming toward her door. Had they come to rob? Then let them take what they wanted and go. Had they come to kill? Or were they drunk and merely wanted shelter? She was getting into her dress when they started pounding on the door with the butts of their muskets.

"Oh, dear God, help! Help me!" Her voice rose shrilly. "What do you want?"

"Open up here! Open up!"

"Go away!"

They were trying to force the door. She heard something about "the Queen's friend. Show her no mercy!"

She thought of leaping from the window but the height was too great and she knew that such a jump would kill her.

She clung to the bedpost, gazing about for some weapon with which to defend herself. It was only a question of time before they succeeded in breaking down the door. She could hear the whines of the loosening iron hinges, the splintering of wood.

"Jerry!" she shrieked. "Jerry!"

Then she realized the distance between his grandmother's cottage and the house.

The men were persistent. The door, heavy as it was, finally fell inward with a crash. For an instant, gasping from their exertion, eight shabby and powerful Roundheads confronted her without movement. Then they came to life again, their eyes roving avidly about the room, while one of them, who looked like a giant, started to move toward her, unmindful of any valuables that that luxurious room might contain. His companions quickly noticed her large jewel case and bounded toward it, snatching it greedily in dirty hands.

"Maid of Honor to the Queen!" cried the giant. "How would it be to kiss the Queen's Maid of Honor?"

"Keep away from me!" she shrieked. "Don't you dare put your hands on me!"

"Must be a fortune in jewels here," exclaimed one of the men.

"This is worth more," said the giant, his eyes upon Hal.

She backed way from him in terror. "Go away. Leave me alone. How dare you——"

He caught her, smothering her words with a long kiss. She squirmed, kicked, pummeled him with her fists, but he only laughed, and while his friends made off with the jewel box, which took two of them to carry, the giant kissed her again.

They were alone in the room now, Hal fighting desperately, but his arms were like a strong vise, and his face, with its stubble of beard and coarse, bulbous lips, began to blur before her. Then he was caught by the shoulders and pulled away.

The man, surprised and off guard, felt himself being wheeled about. Before he could reach for his sword, a fist had caught him on the chin and he fell to the floor, upsetting a small commode. He growled something and tried to rise, but Jerry hit him again and he sank back, lying there motionless with his eyes closed.

Jerry, who had obviously had to fight his way to her, was bleeding from the lip. For an instant he stood there, breathless, legs apart. Then he reached out and caught her by the hand. "Come!"

Her knees were weak and she was sure she was about to collapse. He saw her sway and spoke roughly. "This is no time to faint! Come on!"

He pulled her out into the hall which, since it was windowless, was pitch dark, like the cavern she had seen in her dream.

With one hand moving along the wall to guide him, and the other clasping hers, he ran down the hall toward the rear of the house and the stairs that led to the kitchen. But before reaching them he stopped, for there were sounds of feet running up the front steps and the red glow of torches.

"The linen closet," she whispered. "It's about here somewhere."

With the increasing light of the torches they found the closet and entered it. Shielding her with his body, he shoved her into one corner and closed the door to about five inches just as some men, about ten of them, reached the landing. They passed the closet without seeing it, and Jerry watched as they entered one room after another, putting their torches to the bed canopies, the feather mattresses, the drapes. Then, with smoke spouting simultaneously from every room, they ran down the front stairs where they continued to apply the torch.

"Let all friends of the Queen perish!" one of them cried.

"For God and the liberties of England!" roared another.

"Come," whispered Jerry as soon as the last of them had reached the first floor. "Try not to breathe!"

He clutched her hand again, yanking her from the hiding place, and started for the stairs leading to the kitchen, the only spot where as yet the flames had not reached. But the hall was filled with smoke and it was impossible to see the way.

Before they could find the stairs, Hal stumbled over something and fell, her ankle twisted beneath her. As Jerry tried to pull her to her feet she was deluged with a pain so excruciating that she shrieked.

"I can't—I can't walk!"

The flames were close now, rivulets of flame, almost upon them. She felt him lifting her from the floor and then she fainted.

6 ❊

the revelation

WHEN HAL OPENED HER EYES IT WAS DAYLIGHT AND EVERY-
thing was still. She was in a clean, low-ceilinged, modest
room and a clean, comfortable bed. After a moment of
wonderment she realized where she was. This must be
Cheam's cottage which, hidden from the main house by
tall, thick bushes, had not been invaded. At the thought of
her beloved Langdon Hall being destroyed, she tried to
rise, only to fall back with a moan.

Something had happened to her left leg. When the pain
subsided a bit she realized that the ankle was in splints and
the knee was bandaged. What had happened to her leg?
Would she ever be able to walk again? The suggestion
brought terror. This, coupled with the memory of the
intruders and the fire, was so ghastly that she lay there,
whimpering like a frightened child. The thought came to
her that she was glad her mother had died, for she had been
spared this odious experience.

"Ah, you're awake, my lady." It was Mrs. Cheam, neatly
garbed as usual in a crisply starched linen dress with an
immaculate apron.

80

She sat on the edge of the bed, tenderly smoothing back Hal's hair. "Don't try to move, dear. There. Now you're all right. Just rest quietly. You're lucky it wasn't much worse. There. There."

"If it hadn't been for Jerry—" Hal shuddered at the memory of that burly man with the stubble of beard. "Oh, how much I owe him! Have they gone? Have the men gone?"

"Yes. Nothing to worry about now. Jerry's making you a pair of crutches."

"Crutches! I—I'll have to use crutches?"

"For a while. You've broken your ankle and you seem to have torn a ligament in your knee. But these will heal. In a couple of months you'll walk as good as ever. One must be patient, though."

"I see. I was afraid I was crippled for life. What about Langdon Hall?"

Mrs. Cheam hesitated. "Well, there's no way of keeping it from you. The house and the chimneys, being stone, are still standing. But the roof's gone and the windows are broken. It—it's just a shell—a blackened, ugly shell. Completely gutted. Everything destroyed. Those beautiful paintings of your ancestors, the rugs from Turkey—all gone. The men took the horses and made off with food, jewels, whatever they could carry in their hands. But thank God you're safe!"

"The servants—were any of them . . ."

"One man was killed, two badly wounded. Fortunately all the women got out. They've found shelter in the village. The Roundheads didn't come here to my house at all. Yes, my lady, it might have been much worse."

Her home destroyed, her clothes—her lovely clothes! Those paintings, the exquisite and costly *objets d'art*—all gone. Old things, new things, irreplaceable things. It was not easy to face this fact.

"What—what shall I do?" she asked in a faint, tremulous voice.

"Just get well. You still have the land, the stable, the fish pond, the wells. When your father and brother get back they'll build a new Langdon Hall. Meanwhile, this house is yours. You own it, not I. It's small, but it's shipshape and comfortable."

Hal did not reply. For a long time she lay quietly, trying to comprehend all that Nancy Cheam had said. Langdon Hall destroyed, its many treasures merely ashes. She wanted to cry because of the loss of those lovely things that had made her home a place of luxury and delight. Gone. All gone.

"I know what a shock this is to you," went on Mrs. Cheam sympathetically. "It grieves me, too, for I took great pride in Langdon Hall. But there's no use weeping over yesterday. You're perfectly safe here. Now I'll go and fix you something to eat."

"No, I—I'm not hungry."

"You'll have to eat to get back your strength."

Alone, Hal knew that crying would do no good. She must adjust herself to new conditions, to being bedridden for a time, to living here with Cheam in this one-story stone cottage with its steep roof, raftered ceilings and two stone fireplaces. It contained two small bedrooms, each having space only for a bed, a dresser and one chair; a slightly larger living room and a good-sized kitchen. There were no luxuries. She could not even have a maid. She had no clothes except the dress she had had on when those dreadful men entered her room. She had no jewels. Why, she had not even a brush for her hair!

No, now! She must not let herself sink to the level of self-pity! She would stay here until she was well enough to leave. Meanwhile, she must pay the servants and dismiss them, even her own maids, for there would not be sufficient room to accommodate them here.

Since the vault was below ground, a vast stone cavern, and entered by that secret door which only the family knew, it was unlikely that the intruders had found it or that it had been harmed by the fire.

Half an hour later when Mrs. Cheam returned with the tray, Hal told her where the entrance to the vault was. Would Jerry please go down there and bring up all the bags and boxes?

It was three hours before Jerry, his clothes and hands blackened by soot, brought in one large chest, and having deposited it on the floor near the bed, left the room to return with five heavy bags of gold. He found Hal sitting up, wearing one of his grandmother's nightshifts, her hair neatly combed in two fat braids.

"Sorry I was so long. The door had jammed. That's all of it, my lady."

"Oh, Jerry," she cried feelingly, "how can I thank you for what you've done for me? Why, had it not been for you——"

"I only did what any of your servants would have done, my lady," he replied, embarrassed at her praise and trying not to let her see how inexpressibly dear she was to him. "I'd have gotten to you sooner only I had to tackle several of those fellows first. Sorry you got hurt. I—if you'll excuse me I'll get cleaned up. I was thinking, since your ladyship will be bedridden for a while that you might like me to read to you—say an hour each day."

"Yes, I'd like it very much, but all my books are gone."

"Oh, I've a few you might like. Some I picked up second-hand and some Mr. Milton gave me. I'll be back then, after the midday meal tomorrow, if that meets with your lady-ship's approval?"

"That will be very nice. How kind you are! Jerry, how long will it be before I'm able to walk?"

"Without crutches? I should say at least two—three months, my lady. Is there anything you want now?"

"No. No, thank you. Except—yes. I understand the servants have been taken in by the villagers. Their wages are due and I would like to pay them. Would you find them and have them come to see me tomorrow?"

"Gladly, my lady."

He went out and she gazed after him affectionately, no longer feeling the slightest revulsion because of his dirty hands. Her gratitude was boundless, and relaxing against the pillows she thought, "Oh, he's wonderful!"

Yes, it was true and she candidly admitted it—Jerry Vane was wonderful; wonderfully kind, wonderfully brave, wonderfully strong, wonderfully clever. Was he in love with someone? Certainly all girls must like him. The way they had ogled him at Christmas, shamelessly bidding for his attention! Surely, he must have a sweetheart. This brought an odd pang of sadness. She did not ask herself why, but tried to push the gloomy thought away by beginning to count the gold and silver coins.

To her relief she found that there was enough to pay all the servants, including the large sum she meant to give Mrs. Cheam.

When Hal had made the payments she realized that it would leave her with barely half a bagful of gold. Was it enough to get her to Holland? It was a shock to realize a lack of funds for the first time in her life. Why, what with the loss of her and her mother's jewelry, plus the contents of her home and the immense donations her father had made to the King, the Wades were suddenly poor!

It was a frightening thought. Of course there was considerable income that would be forthcoming from the tenants at the first of the year, but would it be enough to rebuild and refurnish Langdon Hall? No, not nearly. Naturally, if the King won this fight those who had helped him could expect to be generously rewarded, but if he didn't! What would the Wades do? It was impossible to think of any of them actually earning a penny.

"Why, we're a useless, helpless threesome! That's just what we are—useless. What do we have, any of us, to be so proud of? We know how to dance, to sing, to entertain, to ride, to speak French. We're ornamental—and utterly incapable of earning a living! How dreadful!"

Then she remembered that she was betrothed to a man who was reputedly one of the richest in Europe. "I suppose I shall have to marry him now if only to support my father and brother!"

Bleakly, she returned the coins to the bags, and midway she was arrested by the thought that that pot-bellied, unattractive old man might not want to marry her, now that her father could not fulfill the dowry terms.

"So be it. Even if I starve, I'd rather not go through with that marriage!"

She went on putting the coins away and had just finished the task when Nancy Cheam entered.

"My lady, are you still determined to go to the Queen?"

"Yes, Cheam. I promised."

"You could stay here. It's fairly safe now."

"I gave my word. She took only a small retinue with her to Holland and I'm sure she'll need me. As soon as I'm able to travel I must be off. Oh, Cheam, I shall miss you so!"

"Miss me? Why ever should you? I'll soon finish the boy's clothes I started to make for you and you'll travel as my second grandson."

"Your second grandson?"

"Well, it's very plain that Jerry would have to take you to the seaport. Did you think I'd let you go off alone, for heaven's sake? And did you suppose that I could let you and Jerry travel without a chaperon? Your reputation must be protected."

"I—I didn't think of that. Yes, you're right, but to take you away from your nice, cosy home———"

"Now, now. It will be here waiting. If you don't mind my saying so, your ladyship, I love you as much as though you were my own daughter."

"Dear, dear Cheam! And I think you know that next to my own mother I have always loved you."

"Bless you. Oh, my, what a lot of money!"

"There'll be a lot less of it after I've paid off over sixty servants. I'm sorry to have to dismiss them, but what else can I do?"

"I hope your ladyship wasn't planning to dismiss me!"

"You?" Hal smiled brightly. "Oh, never! Mother made us promise that we'd always take care of you. I wish I could give you more, but for the present I want you to take this bag."

"All of that? A whole bagful? Oh, no. I don't need it. I've saved a bit."

"I insist that you take it. I don't want you ever to lack for anything. You've decided to go with me—all the way to Holland?"

"Anywhere."

"Nevertheless, in case we should ever be separated, I

want you to have this money. I shall feel better if I know that no matter what might happen to me you will never be in want. I insist, Cheam. Take it!"

Still Mrs. Cheam hesitated and after a thoughtful moment opened her lips to refuse, but Hal drew her shoulders very straight, lifted her chin and spoke with a decisiveness that reminded Cheam of the Marchioness. "That, my good woman, is an order!"

Nancy Cheam reached out her hand. "Heavens, I never had so much money in my life!"

Hal smiled, relaxed again. "I can never repay you. If I had a million pounds I couldn't possibly repay you for all you've done for me."

"Well, if it makes you feel any better I'll keep it. I've never aspired to the having of wealth. I'm strong and always confident that I can work my way."

Hal sighed. "You're very fortunate. I wish I had that kind of confidence. I wish I'd been trained to be useful. Suddenly I seem helpless and stupid. I couldn't even cook a meal or——"

"Please God you'll never have to. Well, then, as soon as you're able the three of us will be off. I've never been away from this part of England and I've been content here, but I admit there have been times when I thought I'd like to see London."

And so Lady Henrietta Wade, attended only by Nancy Cheam and Jerry Vane, settled down to a long and tedious convalescence. When she had paid off the servants, most of whom were tearful at being dismissed, there was nothing to do but wait for her leg to heal.

If she was idle and inactive her two friends were continuously busy. In addition to doing the washing and cooking, caring for the invalid and cleaning the house, Mrs.

Cheam worked speedily at making two suits of boy's clothes and several nightshifts, cutting down Jerry's shirts to fit Hal and knitting the sort of hose worn by middle-class boys. She took the measurements of Hal's feet and had a pair of boys' shoes made by the village cobbler.

Jerry was busy caring for the herb and vegetable gardens, splitting wood for the fire and bringing water from the well, but he managed to find time each day to read aloud to Hal. When he closed the book he never dallied in the room but made some polite excuse to leave, for Hal's red mouth was inviting and sometimes he wanted so urgently to kiss her, to hold her in his arms and tell her that he loved her, that he stammered awkwardly as he made his excuses to get away.

Shottery remained uninvaded and peaceful during July, with no news from the various fronts. August was stormy. It was as though the elements, like England herself, were in perpetual conflict. Reports drifted in that the royal standard had been raised in Nottingham and the Parliamentary forces under Lord Essex had orders to "follow the King and by battle or other way rescue him from his perfidious councillors and restore him to Parliament," which was simply a diplomatic way of saying, "Arrest him!"

It was during August that the Marquess managed to send word to his daughter. So far he and George were in excellent health and she was to send them, by the messenger who had brought this letter, any money she could spare.

She sent the messenger back with the heartbreaking news of her mother's death and the catastrophe at Langdon Hall. She told of dismissing the servants, of her present position and her determination to join the Queen. She deplored her inability to send them the money they needed, explaining that until someone collected the fees from the tenants,

not due until January, the Wades were practically destitute.

This is a lesson we must learn now, she wrote, *to
do without things. My leg is mending nicely. God
guard you, and may He soon reunite you with*
YOUR LOVING DAUGHTER

In September, limping and using a cane, she started
off with her two devoted companions. Jerry had purchased
an old, spavined horse and a small cart which he filled with
straw.

In this, along with a few boxes of clothes, Mrs. Cheam
and she were to sit while Jerry drove. They must go slowly,
first because they wished to attract as little attention as
possible and second because the aged beast was incapable of
moving in any but a tedious, loping pace. Except when it
was necessary to find lodgings for the night, Jerry chose the
less frequented roads, not knowing from moment to moment whether they would run into a Royalist or Roundhead contingent. But it was an excellent disguise and little
apt to cause undue comment—a frail, invalid, lame boy,
with his grandmother and brother.

Hal looked like a youth of fourteen, shabbily dressed
in ill-fitting, dark clothes. "It's a good thing you must
limp and use that cane," Jerry said, "for ordinarily you've
a girl's walk and I doubt if you could ever fool anyone. But
now—a person would take you for a sort of sickly lad."

"I must look dreadful with my hair cut off."

Actually, she had refused to let him cut it Roundhead
style, but wore it to her shoulders in the Cavalier manner.

After Jerry had used the scissors, when she had looked
down at the floor and seen all that beautiful hair lying

there, she had had difficulty holding back the tears, but after a few days she grew accustomed to having shorter hair and rather liked it.

They talked little on the way, especially to each other. This was Jerry's fault, for he was miserable, knowing that every creaky turn of the wooden wheels was bringing them closer to the time when he must bid farewell, probably forever, to the girl he loved so deeply. It seemed to him that he had always loved her, even when they were little.

Yes, even then he had adored her. Not that he had ever for a moment been fool enough to imagine that Lady Henrietta Wade would ever condescend to marry him. He knew his world too well to entertain a notion so foolish. But she made every other girl seem cheap and uninteresting. All the while he had been at Cambridge she had filled his mind and when he returned to Langdon Hall he had discovered that merely seeing her, talking to her, even being in her vicinity, had brought a zest and brightness to his days.

He was forced to engage in a continual effort not to reveal his feelings, but this he could endure. The hard fact was that now she was going out of the country and that with England in its state of upheaval she might never come back. The time was approaching when she was going out of his life and life without seeing Hal was difficult to contemplate.

So he sat up there on the driver's seat, his back to her and his eyes on the road, and if he spoke at all it was of impersonal matters. "It looks like rain. We'd better stop at the next inn. . . . Sorry, I couldn't avoid that rut. . . . I'm not sure where this road leads. . . ."

He was trying to take as direct a route as possible but detours were inevitable. Having studied a map he knew

the towns they must pass through, or better still, bypass
—Towchester, Wolverton, Ampthill; then a long road to
Cambridge; then Long Melford, Ipswich and on to Felixstone, which he knew to be one of the chosen ports for
ships to and from Holland.

The landscape became monotonous—farm carts; fields
where cows or sheep were browsing; some country women
washing clothes, their tubs set on benches under the trees;
cottages with flowerpots on window sills; henhouses and
paddocks; children playing follow-the-leader; pigeon cotes;
oxen-driven hay carts; water mills; ducks in a stream;
churchbells dimly heard across meadows; morning mists,
chill and somber.

Travelers in England were rarely unable to find some
sort of inn, which inevitably included a landlady who was
both loquacious and inquisitive. Nancy Cheam had a set
little speech that satisfied such a one.

"We're from Worcester and bound for Felixstone where
my elder grandson hopes to find work on the docks. My
younger grandson, poor Hal, he'll never be able to earn a
farthing. Always been kind of shy and delicate, always had
this trouble with his leg. I guess he'll never be what you'd
call brawny. More of the bookish type, that one."

Several times they met a party of Roundheads on their
way to join the Parliamentary forces, but Nancy Cheam and
her two grandsons excited no suspicion. They met with a
minor difficulty, however, one afternoon when they were
on the outskirts of Wolverton and they came upon a dozen
Roundheads lounging in a grove of gnarled oaks. They
might have gone on their way peacefully had not one of
the rear wheels of the dilapidated cart chosen that time to
come off.

Jerry stopped, climbed down from his perch and managed to fix it, the men, bored and weary, coming close to watch him and to call out advice.

One of them peered into the cart. "Ho!" he cried. "We've a Cavalier here!"

"The likes of us—Cavaliers!" retorted Mrs. Cheam briskly. "We're decent country people minding our own business and I'll thank you to do the same."

"If you don't like being taken for Cavaliers, you'd better give that young lad a haircut."

Jerry spoke soothingly. "Leave him alone. He's only thirteen and vain of his hair. My grandmother and I often tease him about it. Well, the wheel's fixed. We'll be on our way. How far is it to Ampthill?"

The men seemed not to hear him. They were looking at Hal, sitting there on the straw, her shoulders hunched, her eyes wide with apprehension.

"Come here, lad," said one of the men goodnaturedly; and reaching in his knapsack, he took out a pair of shears. "What do you say," he asked his companions laughingly, "if I give the boy a haircut?"

This idea seemed to amuse them. "Yes. If he's no Cavalier he shouldn't go around looking like one."

"You keep your hands off my grandson," exclaimed Nancy. "He's sickly and his leg's painful."

"They mean no harm," said Jerry. "Better humor them."

"Come on down, sonny. What you need's a haircut."

"No!" cried Hal. "No, an it please you—no!"

Jerry laughed as though sharing the men's amusement. "Don't he sound like a girl, though? Come on, Hal, the men won't hurt you." Obediently Hal climbed down from the cart. "That's right. You're not a child any more. Time you started acting like a man." He turned to the men. "If you must give my little brother a haircut, don't cut it too close, for there'll be no living with him if you do. My grandmother's spoiled him because he's poorly." In a gesture of fraternal affection he flung his arm about Hal's shoulders. "It's all right with you, boy?"

She made herself smile. "It—it's all right."

By the time the men had snipped off her hair it no longer fell to her shoulders, but clustered close to her head in ringlets.

"I swear, Hal," said Jerry when the operation was over, "that's better. Get back into the cart and we'll be on our way." He waved his hand cheerily to the men. "Good fortune to you, my friends, and good luck to the cause!" He gave the rallying cry of the Parliamentarians, "God with us."

They responded genially with the answer. "For God and the liberties of England!"

When they were on their way, Jerry said quietly, "I congratulate you on your wise deportment, my lady. We might have had trouble there. They were on the verge of turning nasty."

Her voice was tearful. "Oh, my poor hair! I must look a sight. Everyone will laugh at me in Holland."

"There now," said Mrs. Cheam, "when they know the circumstances they'll commend you. As a matter of fact, it looks quite nice. I like it that way."

On they went, through small villages where houses were no higher than two storys, most of them with rose vines around the front doors which opened directly on the narrow, unpaved lanes; down winding, rutty byways; past tall hawthorn hedges; through forests; over stone bridges spanning brooks.

So far the weather had been kind to them, but now it

began to rain, making the way muddy. There was one night when the rain increased to such a downpour that they found refuge in a barn. Next morning when it had subsided to a drizzle they took to the road again, soaked and uncomfortable.

From time to time housewives and farmers would call out, "Any news of the war?"

They shook their heads regretfully.

As they rode, Hal lay back on the straw, folding her arms behind her head, eyes closed against the glare of the sun. Since Nancy was anything but an idle chatterer, Hal had much time for thinking during that journey. She knew that once Jerry had seen her aboard some ship for Holland she might never meet him again, for he was determined to enlist in the Parliamentary forces.

This knowledge produced in Hal an inner struggle, for in her mind it was wrong—it was actually treason—to fight against the King. She knew, then, that she ought to despise him, for there was nothing in the world so despicable as a traitor; yet somehow this seemed completely apart from Jerry himself, from her dependence upon him and the reliance she placed in him. It was all very confusing, producing an inner battle that brought only unhappiness and bafflement.

The thought that she might be in love with him had not occurred to her. She only knew that being isolated from him, perhaps forever, was unbearably painful. She tried to steel herself against the moment of parting by thinking about the King and the difficulties Parliament had placed him in.

She was sure that it was all Parliament's fault and that the King's stand was a righteous one. God had ordained

him to rule, and rule he should. Frequently the words of
Milton came to her:

A crown, golden in show, is but a wreath of thorns;
Brings dangers, troubles, cares and sleepless nights
To him who wears the royal diadem,
When on his shoulders each man's burden lies;
For therein stands the office of a king,
His honor, virtue, merit and chief praise,
That for the public all this weight he bears.

What a weight their Majesties were bearing now! She
did not resent the fact that her father had given almost all
his wealth to the crown. She was filled with compassion for
the royal couple and only regretted that there was not more
to give.

Having taken roundabout paths to avoid highways, they
did not reach Cambridge until late October. This city was
a Puritan stronghold. One saw only Roundheads on the
streets. It was fifty-six miles from London, a market town
as well as a center for universities. Mrs. Cheam decided that
since they were sure to find excellent accommodations at an
inn, they would have to stay here at least two days, for not
only did they need rest but she had a great deal of launder-
ing to do. Hal, she said, was to remain in the room—and
they must take the cheapest they could find.

"Now that you hardly limp at all, anyone could tell that
you're not a boy. It would be risky for you to be seen on
the street. Besides, some of these Parliamentarians might
have seen you with the Queen. So it's best that you stay in
the room and I shall say that my younger grandson is not
well."

Hal nodded humbly.

"And I," said Jerry, "will spend these few days with my old master, John Milton."

The thought of getting away from Hal seemed to him an almost heaven-sent protection. It had been comparatively easy to conceal his feelings when they were driving along and he had sat with his back to her, but now—no. Two days at the inn and he would be sure to break down and act like a lovesick fool. And he'd be a fool indeed to reveal his affection for her.

Life had been cruel. It had placed them immeasurably apart from one another. There was no more likelihood of his ever marrying Lady Henrietta Wade than there was of his flying to the moon. *So be careful, be watchful.* While being with her was a sweet torment and the thought of final parting brought anguish, better never to get too close to her, never to be alone with her, never let her suspect what a presumptuous idiot he was.

So, having found a room for Hal and his grandmother at an inexpensive inn, he took abrupt leave of them and walked rapidly to the modest house of his friend, trying not to think of what might happen if any of these Roundheads knew that in the midst of them was the girl known to have been a close companion of the Queen.

In the room she shared with Mrs. Cheam, Hal stood at the mullioned window, not having to use the cane now, and watched Jerry pensively as he strode down the crowded street. Her companion was unpacking, sorting the many things to be washed.

"Are you homesick for Langdon Hall?" Hal asked.

"Sometimes a little, though I thank God we've come this far without any trouble. It's cold in here. That's a Tudor fireplace and they never give out much heat. So much the better. Gives you an excuse to be in bed when the maid comes to bring the towels. Cover yourself up and have a book to read. Hmm. Quite a load to be washed. Well, there's a good, honest wind—fine weather for drying."

Mrs. Cheam picked up the laundry and left. Hal took off her shoes, doublet and breeches, donning one of Jerry's nightshifts, which Nancy had altered to fit her. She was growing accustomed now to dressing and undressing without assistance and she had even learned to hang up her clothes.

She had just climbed into bed when there was a knock on the door. In a voice which she made as deep as possible she called, "Come in," and a frowsy maid appeared, bringing a fresh pitcherful of water and two grayish towels.

"What's the news of the war?" asked Hal.

"They say the King has moved his forces to Shrewsbury and his army has gotten stronger. Prince Rupert's with him. He means to take London, but there's no chance of that. Lord Essex is now moving to Worcester. Oh, he'll protect London, all right! We won't let the King get within miles of it."

Hal opened the book to hide her face, which she knew must reveal joy at the word that the King's forces were increasing.

Staying cooped up in that room began to bore her after a while and next evening she was relieved when Mrs. Cheam brought in the laundry, all carefully ironed, and said they would be moving on the next day.

At Ipswich Jerry learned that a boat was sailing from Felixstone for Holland in ten days. This meant that they must waste no time. But the cart had again broken down and it required a day to fix it. The tired old horse looked reproachfully at him as Jerry began to harness him.

Ipswich was seething with excitement. The first important battle of the war had taken place on the twenty-third of October at Edgehill. Though it was really a drawn battle, the King claimed the victory. The Cavaliers had plainly outfought the Roundheads. The King had withdrawn to Warwick. His advisers were urging him not to attempt to take London but to establish his headquarters at Oxford.

Since Warwick was not far from Shottery, Hal imagined the unhappiness that her father and brother would be suffering when they saw what had happened to Langdon Hall. That is, if they were still alive. She often found herself worrying about them and at times the uncertainty seemed unbearable.

"Thousands of women are going through that same thing," said Mrs. Cheam. "I think in a war it's the women who suffer most. I know how I shall feel when Jerry joins the army."

"Jerry! Oh, dear, something else I shall have to worry about!"

"I'm honored," said Jerry sarcastically, his eyes on the road, "that her ladyship would condescend to worry about a mere servant. Why, in her eyes I'm little more than scum; besides, to her mind, I deserve death since she considers me a traitor."

"All the same," replied Hal in an unsteady voice, "I wouldn't want anything to happen to you. I—I consider you one of my best friends. I owe you a great deal. I'm not quite heartless, you know."

They were entering Felixstone now. Jerry, silent as usual, drove the two women to an inn and, after Hal had given him money for the passage, hurried off to arrange a reservation for Lady Henrietta Wade and her maid. He returned with the information that everything was fixed and the boat would sail in an hour. He found that Hal had discarded the ill-fitting boy's suit and had changed into the only dress she had—the black satin that she had worn when the Roundheads had burst into her room. Never had she looked lovelier.

"We're in luck," said Mrs. Cheam, who seemed curiously blind to the emotions the two young people were undergoing, "to be sailing so soon and with no difficulty."

But Hal did not feel that it was luck at all. In fact, she stood there staring into space as though suddenly stricken. To leave him—why, it was like tearing her heart out! Her eyes filled with tears.

"Jerry," she begged, "you—you'll take good care of yourself? Oh, don't get shot or anything!"

The sight of those big, dark eyes swimming in tears was almost more than Jerry could bear. He forced himself to smile as he busied himself tying the rope around a single box which constituted all the luggage belonging to Hal and her "grandmother."

"I shall do my best, my lady."

"After I've been your 'brother' for so long, it—it doesn't seem right f-for you to—to call me 'my lady' so formally."

He was still busy with the box and neither of them noticed how awkward his fingers were.

"That's the way it must be, ma'am. You are my lady. I am your humble servant. It can never be any other way."

She turned away to the window while Mrs. Cheam kissed him fondly, saying their farewells now rather than at the dock. Hal, confused and hurt, stared unseeingly at the street. Yes, he was right. That was how it must be and it could never be any other way—and yet in this moment when the pain of parting was keen and merciless, she awakened sharply to the fact that she loved Jerry Vane and she would never love anyone else!

"Well, come," Mrs. Cheam was saying. "We'd best be

starting. We'll walk to the boat, to save money. Anyhow, it's only a few blocks. My, it's a pleasant day for sailing!"

A pleasant day for sailing! To Jerry and Hal it was a day of distress, a bleak and terrible day, wherein hearts were silently breaking. Determined not to give way to any show of emotion, Hal walked by the side of Nancy Cheam while Jerry followed behind with the box. It seemed no time at all before they were at the gangplank and Nancy turned to her grandson for a last quick kiss, begging him to wear his muffler now that it was fall. Then she took the box from him and hastened up the gangplank.

Hal and Jerry faced each other.

"Well, good-by, my lady," he said, trying to speak jauntily. "A pleasant voyage. Perhaps you'll soon return, since the King's cause seems to be prospering."

Suddenly the King's cause meant nothing to her. She longed for one thing—to reach out and cling to him and kiss him and feel his arms about her.

"All aboard," came a command from the ship. "All aboard!"

Fearing to speak lest words betray her, Hal looked at him long and tenderly. His face was white and she realized that he, too, was suffering. In that poignant moment of revelation their eyes said what their lips dared not, and each knew how boundless was their mutual love.

"All aboard!" came that cruel, insistent voice again.

Hal turned and walked up the gangplank, not daring to look back lest she rush impetuously into his arms.

He stood watching as she walked onto the deck and disappeared, not being sufficiently strong to wave at him from the rail, but only wanting to be alone and face the wonder and the torment that engulfed her.

"Good-by—my love," he muttered brokenly.

7 ❀

the new duchess

IT WAS, INDEED, FAVORABLE WEATHER FOR SAILING. THE
sea was smooth as a pond and the little ship made excellent time. On arriving in Holland they discovered that
the Queen was at the Hague and they lost no time in getting there.

Her Majesty had been in Holland since February. Eight
months had gone by since she had left her husband on
the Dover shore, watching the ship sail away, his eyes filled
with tears. At the Hague the royal visitor had been received by Henry, Prince of Orange. To him she explained
her real reason for coming. It was not to be courted and
feasted. It was to sell her jewels and borrow from the
burghers in order to buy munitions and weapons that her
husband might carry on what she called "this righteous
war." After turning her ten-year-old daughter, Princess
Mary, over to the care of the child's future mother-in-law,
Queen Mary at once plunged into the all-important business of accomplishing her mission.

She took a house, small by comparison with those palaces
she had lived in in England, but sufficiently large to accom-

modate her retinue, which consisted of her faithful dwarf, Jeffrey Hudson; two priests; several chamberwomen; pages; eight ladies-in-waiting, each of whom had one or two maids; and about twenty officers, none of whom would have thought of leaving England without at least three personal servants.

When Hal was announced, Mary was in a large reception room surrounded by her ladies. She gave a gasp of joy and ordered the girl to be shown in at once. Hal entered and knelt.

"Ah, *ma chère!*" cried the Queen, arms outstretched. "You have kept your word. *Comment allez-vous?* How are you? Ah, your hair! What has happen to your lovely hair? Sit down. Tell me the news."

The Queen seemed not to have aged a day. Anxiety had not dimmed her vivaciousness. She was truly a beautiful woman, with her slender, oval face, dark, curly hair and perfectly-formed mouth. As usual she was tastefully gowned in a heavy satin dress trimmed at the neck and sleeves with frail lace.

Hal began by telling what she knew of the King's movements and the victory he had claimed at Edgehill.

"Ah," sighed Mary, "how I long to see him! But now tell us of yourself. You are thinner, *non?* And ah, your poor hair!"

With the ladies listening attentively, Hal told of the departure of her father and brother to join the King, and her mother's death. She went on to tell of the invasion of Langdon Hall, its destruction and the injury to her leg. The ladies sighed and shook their heads.

"*Quelle honte!*" gasped Mary. "Who would have believed it! Go on."

There was the story of her ride in the hay cart disguised

as a boy, with her two faithful servants, the meeting with the band of Roundheads, the cutting of her hair.

"So that's the story, madam. I have no money, no jewels and what's worse, I have only the gown I'm wearing, but here I am."

"Do not worry, *ma petite*. Madame la Comtesse Carlyle?"

"Yes, your Majesty?"

"You must see that her ladyship gets the clothes she needs. We will all contribute, eh?"

"Gladly, madam."

"You have nothing to worry, *ma petite*. Oh, and you will be glad to hear that Monsieur le Duc, your fiance, is with us."

"The Duke of Thewes—here? Now?"

"*Oui*. When he hears I am in Holland he comes to be of assistance to me. But now you must excuse me. Some burghers are arriving. I must see the gentlemen. Oh, my lady Hal, I am rejoicing! Every day they lend me more money! *Le croyez-vous?* It is wonderful!"

As the Queen left the room her ladies knelt. Then they all crowded around Hal, telling her how brave she was and promising to bring her what clothes they could spare. As every one of them had extensive wardrobes, in two hours Hal had more clothes than she could ever possibly need, and Nancy was busily altering them.

Her ladyship was given a small, simple room where a cot had been placed for the older woman. There was scant time for amusements, for the Queen proclaimed proudly that she was there on business and she attended to it without respite. Her business was to charm the wealthy Dutch burghers into giving her or lending her their money.

Soon after breakfast next morning the Duke had himself

announced. Hal decided to receive him in her bedroom, since it was only there that she could talk with any degree of privacy. Mrs. Cheam sat sewing industriously in the far corner as he entered, pompous, elegantly dressed, his graying hair curled and perfumed, his fat hands gleaming with rings.

"My lady," he said with a bow.

"Your Grace," she replied, curtsying.

"I've heard of the dreadful things you've had to face since I last saw you. I must commend you for your courage and stamina."

"Thank you, sir. I'm sorry I have to receive your Grace in my bedroom, but I wanted to talk to you without fear of interruption. Please be seated." She motioned stiffly to a chair across from her.

"I'm pleasured. What? Have you become a Roundhead?" Considering this remark extremely comic, he laughed heartily.

Hal waited politely until his merriment subsided. On the boat she had faced the fact that she loved Jerry Vane, loved him wholly, but she knew marriage was impossible; her father would never consent to it, and even if by some miracle he should, marriage would still be impossible. It was not because Jerry's station in life was lowly, not because he was poor, but even though she might be brave enough to flaunt custom and be snubbed by her friends, she was totally unfitted to be the wife of a man like Jerry Vane.

It was impossible to imagine herself scrubbing floors, mending, washing, cooking. No, she was not the right wife for Jerry.

But though she could not marry him, her love for him

made the idea of marrying the Duke so repulsive that she decided to take matters in her own hands and break off her betrothal. Rightly, this should have been done by her father, but her father was not here; besides, a plight-troth was legally almost as binding as a marriage and it could not be severed save by mutual agreement.

"Your Grace," she began when his laughter subsided, "if you have heard of all that has happened to me you must be aware that my father will no longer be able to fulfill the contract as to my dowry."

"Hmm. I hadn't thought of that. Yes, quite so."

"So since my father is not here, I ask you—I beg you—to terminate the troth!"

"Eh? What? What?"

This man was accustomed to being flattered and humored. It seemed to Hal that now his thin eyebrows shot all the way up to his hairline. He simply could not believe that this girl, whose position at court was far inferior to his own and who had just confessed to being practically a pauper, would be asking him to set her free. Then he smiled indulgently.

"Oh, I see. It's your pride. We-ell, I am willing to forego the dowry."

He expected her to overwhelm him with appreciation, but his generous announcement left her unmoved.

"Your Grace is kind, but I beg you not to forego it! I don't love you and I'm sure I never could. So I beg you to release me."

He realized that she was painfully sincere. "Love?" he asked. "Love? What has love to do with this? We shall get on well enough. Never fear. You'll not find me too exacting."

"Why should your Grace wish to hold me to this contract? There are many ladies at court who, I'm sure, would be more suitable."

"Perhaps. However, I chose you. And now that we are being so unpleasantly frank, I confess that I am determined to marry. She must be a woman who is young enough and healthy enough to outlive me. Let me explain. At present my sole heir is my younger brother with whom I have always been at loggerheads. Now that the cad has joined Essex's forces the feud between us is intensified. A traitor, a scoundrel. Knowing that I have no other heirs, he is only waiting for me to die, actually hoping for my death. Well, I have sworn that I will fool him. Not a farthing of mine must he get! When I marry—and since I am in excellent health there is no hurry about that—I shall see to it that all my property is left to my wife."

"Then you intend to hold me to the contract merely to spite a brother whom you hate?"

"That is one reason—yes. You are young and certain to outlive him. Another reason is that I'm sure in time I could grow fond of you; besides, there's no other woman of suitable rank whose beauty can compare with yours. I like to be proud of the things I own. There you have the truth, my lady. Now we understand each other."

His eyes wandered to the far corner where Nancy was engrossed in her sewing and apparently paying no attention to the conversation. "It seems you owe a great deal to this worthy woman. After we're married I will reward her well for taking such excellent care of you."

Mrs. Cheam gave him a modest smile as she knotted her thread.

"Sir," begged Hal feelingly, "let me go. I—I'm in love with someone else."

He shrugged. "You're young. You'll get over that. Well, I must go now. I'm extremely busy, you know. I must see some burghers on behalf of the Queen. I am able to advise her as to how much to spend for ammunition, how much to spend for weapons and what kind to buy. It is a difficult assignment. Many soldiers still prefer the bow to this new contraption, the musket. Too, much of the fighting is done with swords and pikes; seventeen or eighteen feet long, those pikes, deadly weapons. Fortunately, armor was given up in the time of James, so that is one thing less to be considered. The Queen graciously accepts my advice in these matters. An admirable woman. The Dutch are quite charmed with her. She handles them tactfully. Our ambassador has been instructed by Parliament to thwart her purposes at all costs, but because of her beauty and charm he has been unable to accomplish anything."

"Parliament knows what she is doing here, then?"

"Oh, perfectly. And they'll know when she leaves. They'll use every means in their power to prevent her from getting those valuable arms to the King."

"May I ask, when we return to England will your Grace be among our company?"

"I shall see my liege-lady safely to England and then I shall at once return to France. I would make a poor soldier. Not built for it, you know. The King is better off without me. Besides, a battle is a messy affair and I abhor messiness."

"Has her Majesty been able to acquire a great deal of money to buy these weapons?"

"It's amazing, what she has accomplished! Do you know that their High Mightinesses of Rotterdam have lent her forty thousand guilders? The Bank of Amsterdam has lent her eight hundred and forty-five thousand more. On her pendant pearls alone she has borrowed two hundred and thirteen thousand two hundred guilders. Altogether she had managed to raise two million pounds sterling! And all of it is being put into arms. If she succeeds in getting these to the King, our cause is probably won."

"Oh, this is wonderful news! But, your Grace, returning to the marriage contract, I beg you to reconsider."

"I promise nothing but to think about it," he replied coldly.

His Grace bowed and left. Hal paced the floor wretchedly. "He's fatter and older than when I saw him last. Red-faced, overdressed—ugh!"

"Now, calm down, your ladyship," said Nancy. "You might do worse. I'm sure the Duke is well meaning. And remember, when you marry him you'll be the richest woman in Europe. You're not apt to find a better husband, especially since he generously foregoes your dowry."

"Money doesn't matter much any more, Cheam."

"It behooves you to be sensible. It's your duty to think of your father." Nancy glanced at the clock. "It's your time to be on duty. You must go to the Queen. Here. This gown is finished now. Let me help you put it on, and if your ladyship will forgive me for saying so, a little rouge wouldn't be amiss."

Fifteen minutes later when Hal entered the Queen's apartment she found Mary standing at the window, frowning. Mitte, asleep on one of the upholstered chairs, looked up at the newcomer and growled.

"Come in *m'amie. Mon Dieu!* How homesick I am for England! Yet I know the people wish to separate me from my lord, the King. Indeed, Parliament has publicly declared it is necessary to do this. *Ma foi,* they have even announced that as Queen I am only a subject and am amenable like other persons, and now I hear that they have publicly accused me by name! *Oui! C'est vrai!*"

"I know, madam."

"*Écoutez!* They accuse me of having wished to overthrow the laws and religion of the kingdom! They say it was I who caused the Irish to revolt. They even have witnesses to swear to that! *Il sont imaginé des choses fausses.* Pray for me, Hal. It is a sad thing. In all the world is no creature more wretched than I—separated from my lord the King and from my children—out of my country without hope of returning there except at great peril!"

"But you have accomplished wonders in Holland, madam, and when you join the King, bringing so much to aid him in his righteous fight, the war will surely end speedily. We are all immensely proud of you. May I ask when your Majesty plans to return?"

"Soon, I hope. As soon as I finish my business here. *Hélas!* My children are in the care of Parliament and I shall not be able to see them, but I shall see my husband! *Oui*, we shall go back as soon we can."

But it was not until February 2 that they sailed from Scheveling. The royal party, that day, was all in a gay and confident mood. The hold of the ship and the holds of eleven others were filled with ammunition. The Queen was proud of herself, certain of ultimate triumph.

Hal had seen little of her fiance during those three months, for he worked hard in the Queen's service. In the house he had rented, he had given sumptuous dinners every evening to any burghers who might be of use to her Majesty. Daytimes he had interviewed makers of muskets, pikes and ammunition, and bargained shrewdly as well as urging haste in their manufacture. Hal was forced to admit that though he frankly confessed that he would not fight, he had served wisely in another and an equally important way. She doubted that he had had any time to decide whether or not to hold her to the marriage contract.

Did the Parliamentary forces know of the Queen's departure from Holland? Was there danger in this voyage? But the Queen's ladies and her officers felt safe knowing that their ship was followed by eleven others, and convoyed by the Dutch admiral, Van Tromp. They soon discovered, however, that there were dangers other than an opposing army.

For nine terrifying days a ferocious gale tossed the ships about as though they were toys. Death, it seemed, could be expected at any moment. With the exception of Hal and Queen Mary everyone, even the priests, was wretchedly seasick. Most of the time the whole party had to be tied in their bunks, since any movement was perilous. The Queen's ladies, dignity forgotten, wept and screamed and called wildly for the priests, who were so seasick that they could scarcely lift their heads. Through it all the Queen's mood remained buoyant.

"Do not be afraid," she repeated laughingly. "Never has a Queen of England been killed at sea!"

Hal, though frightened, was the only one able to attend her Majesty and though they were unable to move about, they often sat close to one another in the cabin, confiding in each other. Mary talked of her life in France as a girl and of her headstrong behavior during those first months in England. Hal, because she could not get Jerry out of her mind, told of all he had done for her and how on that day of parting she had suddenly awakened to the startling fact that she loved him.

"It is ridiculous, *ma chère*," replied Mary lightly. "You must forget him. *Oui. Vraiment.* Forget him."

"I shall never be able to do that, your Majesty."

"You would marry him? *Non!* That cannot be. Never. *Fi donc!* That you should give your heart to a Roundhead and a mere servant. Impossible!"

"I realize that. It's quite impossible. But I know that he loves me and I shall never cease to love him. I cannot marry the Duke."

"You are very foolish. I will order you to marry him, for this will save you from making a big mistake. So soon as we are settled I shall order that the marriage take place. *Voyons!* Don't be angry. What I do is for your good."

Finally the boat was driven back to Holland, dropping anchor not far from where they had started. After two days of rest, with everyone except Hal and Mary so weak that they had to stay in bed, the ladies and gentlemen of the Queen's retinue dragged themselves to the dock. This time they had a pleasant voyage and reached Burlington Bay on the twentieth. Though everyone was eager to go ashore, the Duke prevailed upon the Queen to remain aboard until a sufficient escort could reach her.

The King had received news of her return, and though he himself was unable to meet her he had promised to send an escort to protect her on her journey to Oxford. As for the Duke, Burlington Bay, he said, was as far as he intended to go. The boat that had carried him from Holland would take him back there as soon as he had seen the Queen safely on her way. Two days after their arrival he and the Queen were at the rail, eagerly watching for the royal escort.

"My friend," said her Majesty gravely, "you should name the day of your marriage."

"Pardon, your Majesty, but I can scarcely do that without a conference with the Marquess."

"As you wish, but I order you to lose no time in this matter. I—" she broke off, and her dark, vivacious eyes lighted up with excitement. *"Regardez!* They are here!"

One thousand Cavaliers were marching toward the ship and at sight of her they broke into one of the rallying cries of the Royalists. "God for Queen Mary!"

She walked ashore, smiling at them, and presently Hal, who was behind her, gave a gasp of joy, for George was among them. He first had to kneel before his Queen, giving her some important information. The King was at Oxford, where she was to join him with all possible speed. Oxford, like London, was well fortified. Prince Rupert had captured Brentford in November. The ammunition was badly needed.

When the Queen had dismissed him George turned to embrace his sister. Yes, he said in reply to her query, Father was alive and well. But George could not talk long. Wagons had to be found to transport the ammunition and luggage and he had to help in overseeing the unloading.

Meanwhile, the Queen and her retinue had taken shelter in a large house near the bay, where her Majesty intended to remain until the huge amount of ammunition could be unloaded and packed and an even larger escort arrived.

Everyone was in high spirits as they retired that night. They were back in England and their loved ones were awaiting them at Oxford. With the ammunition, Charles was sure to win and all the nasty business would soon be over.

That morning at dawn they were aroused by the thunder of cannon. When Nancy had helped Hal to dress, the girl ran at once to the Queen, entering the royal chamber unceremoniously. All the other ladies were hysterical. Mary was sitting up in bed, her eyes frenzied, staring in the direction from which the shots had come.

Hal grabbed the Queen's hand and yanked her to the floor. "Get up, your Majesty! Quick! Put on your clothes. They're certainly concentrating on this house. They know you're here!"

The shots were coming faster now. The Queen was half dressed when Jeffrey Hudson came in followed by George and the Duke.

"Get the Queen out of here!" roared his Grace, his face purple with excitement.

"*Que faire?*" cried Mary as Hal buttoned her dress. "What's to be done? Where shall I go?"

"Get out!" cried George. "Get out! Five ships of war entered Burlington Bay during the night. You were known to be asleep in this house. They have spies everywhere. They're concentrating all their efforts on this place!"

"I'm ready. We go. Give me your hand. Come! But where we go?"

George took her hand and led her down the stairs and out into the street where panic-stricken people were racing in all directions, houses were being demolished on all sides and half-dressed women were screaming and fainting. Followed by several attendants, the Queen was running by George's side when suddenly she broke away from him and to the consternation of her attendants raced back into the house she had just left. Hal and George ran after her.

"Is she mad?" cried George. "Your Majesty, no!"

But she kept going while the cannon roared about her. Entering the house, she dashed up the stairs and grabbed Mitte, who was asleep on her bed. Holding the small animal close to her, she raced down the stairs again.

"Your Majesty risks her life and ours for that ugly little dog!" exclaimed the Duke furiously.

"*Prenez garde!*" she called. "Where we go?"

No one answered. A servant was killed only a few feet from her, but they stepped over him and kept running. The bombardment continued with increased fury.

Because she had brought arms for her husband, Parliament had voted Mary guilty of high treason, and its sole idea was to kill her. As Mary and her party raced to a trench outside of town the shots roared about them, missing them by inches. At last they reached a ditch where the rest of her retinue were cowering. They stumbled into it, and the enemy forces, as though with diabolical inspiration, aimed at that precise spot. Again and again cannon balls grazed its edge and scattered dirt over the quaking Royalists, some of whom were praying incoherently. In the Bay, the valiant Van Tromp was doing all in his power to defend the Queen, and finally, but not until midmorning when the firing had continued for four hours, he succeeded in driving away the Parliamentary ships.

Suddenly everything was quiet. In the main street houses opposite the one in which Mary had taken refuge were entirely demolished. The streets were littered with bodies, some dead, some badly wounded. The royal party, disheveled, dirt-covered, gazed at one another dazedly.

"What we do now?" asked Mary. "Where we go? Let's get out of this ditch. What's to be done?"

It was only then that they discovered that the Duke of Thewes was unconscious and had been badly wounded. Some of the men lifted him out of the trench and put him on the ground while they conferred as to where they would go.

There might be another attempt on the Queen's life and that house was too close to the Bay for safety. George remembered Boynton Hall, a large manor outside Burlington which belonged to staunch Royalists. After sending their servants back to the house near the Bay to get their possessions, the bedraggled Royalists started toward Boynton Hall, while George went to find a wagon to transport the Duke.

Despite her non-regal appearance, Mary was far from depressed. "You see?" she cried excitedly, still holding the dog, "God has preserved us!"

They were received at Boynton Hall with all ceremony. The Duke was given a large, airy room and the doctor was sent for. At once the Queen sent a letter to her husband telling him what had happened and saying that she would remain at least ten days until her ladies had sufficiently recovered to proceed.

The doctor, harrassed by the many urgent calls on his services, was sure that the Duke would recover. Yes, it was a bad wound but not necessarily fatal.

His Grace had four menservants, all of whom were inept and bungling when it came to caring for an invalid. Mrs. Cheam, sizing up the situation, took charge. Her motherly soul went out to the poor, suffering creature and she treated him not as his Grace the Duke of Thewes but as though he were a small, badly behaved boy.

"Get out of here!" he roared. "I'll not be bathed by a woman and I'll not be bossed like this! Who do you think you are, telling me what to eat and what to do?"

"Quiet, now. I'm here to do what I can. Your wound is badly inflamed and bursting into a temper will only inflame it the more."

Calmly and efficiently she fed him, bathed him, cleansed the ugly wound in his arm which, because of gangrene, was giving off a foul odor. Night after night she sat up with him and at first she was sure she could save him. No longer did he roar at her, threatening to have her killed if she did not leave him alone.

"Your Mrs. Cheam is a fine woman," he said one day when Hal came to call on him. "I intend to reward her."

"She's not doing this for a reward, your Grace. Cheam is the sort who just has to take care of people."

"Kitteredge," he spoke to one of his servants who was standing by looking helpless and worried, "bring me my strongbox."

When the box had been brought, he opened it, fished among some papers, finally handing one of them to Hal. She saw that it was the marriage contract which had been signed by her father and himself.

"Tear it up," he ordered.

"Oh, sir, you're most kind!"

"Tear it up, I said!" he watched as she obeyed. "Now we're both free." His face against the pillow looked pasty and swollen. "But by heaven, my money shall not go to my brother! You say I'm kind, my lady? I'm not. I'm a selfish, stubborn old man. Not a cent will he get from me! Not a cent!"

"Don't think of that now," said Nancy. "Think only of getting well. Lie still. It's time I put a new dressing on your——"

"Don't bother. I'm not going to live. Kitteredge, fetch me one of her Majesty's priests. Go on! Don't stand staring!"

"A priest?" asked Mrs. Cheam. "Whatever would you be wanting with him? To make a confession, is it? Absolution? Now, now, you're not going to die."

"Don't argue with me, woman! I want a priest!"

Humoring him as she would a child, she motioned

116

Kitteredge to obey, and then she changed the bandage. He moaned, cursed, and closed his eyes. When she had drawn the covers tenderly about him, she said gently, "Try to sleep now. I'll just put this cold rag on your head. So soothing."

"I don't want a rag on my head. How can you soothe a man when he's dying?"

"Now, now, you're not——"

He looked at Hal. "You stay here. I'm going to need you."

He dropped off to sleep, but his eyes opened quickly when Kitteredge entered half an hour later with the priest.

"Come in, sir," said Mrs. Cheam cheerily. "The poor dear thinks he's about to die and wishes to make a confession."

"Confession nothing!" replied his Grace irritably. "I'll not leave a penny to my rascal of a brother. You are going to marry me, my good woman, here and now!"

"Oh," said the priest, "this is most un——"

"I think he must be delirious!" gasped Hal.

"No, I'm not!" cried the Duke furiously. "I know perfectly well what I'm doing. Call witnesses. It must be done properly."

"Cheam," began Hal, "the Duke is——"

"Now, now," said Mrs. Cheam, "he must not be angered. Excitement will only bring more inflammation to that wound. But your Grace, you really shouldn't be doing this. I'm only a serving woman. I've no wish to step out of my class."

"Stop chattering," ordered the invalid. "Get on with it, my man. What other witnesses do you need?"

"Well, er—Kitteredge and Lady Hal will be sufficient. But this is most irregular and——"

"Don't excite him, I beg of you," said Nancy, "unless you wish to answer for his life. We can have it annuled later."

"Please join hands," said the priest, obviously upset. "Now. Your first names?"

"Nancy," said Mrs. Cheam, looking suddenly distraught.

"William James Henry—" mumbled the Duke.

So, with Kitteredge and Hal as witnesses, Mrs. Cheam became the Duchess of Thewes, a title which gave her precedence at court even above Hal.

"Oh, my goodness!" she gasped when the priest had finally left. Then she turned to her unruly patient. "Now it's over. Try to relax." She felt of his forehead. "Your fever's up again. Tch! Kitteredge, bring some cold water and some goat's milk with an egg shaken up in it, and send someone for the doctor."

"Never mind that," the Duke spoke in a tone of authority. "The doctor's a fool. Kitteredge, fetch me a lawyer and waste no time about it!"

Kitteredge seemed stupefied. "A—a lawyer, your Grace?"

"Do as he says," advised Mrs. Cheam. Then, to her new husband, "but whatever in the world do you want a lawyer for?"

The Duke seemed not to be listening. He was grinding his teeth in an effort to stifle his moans. Mrs. Cheam shook her head worriedly at Hal, but before she could speak, the room began to be filled with noble personages, for Kitteredge had blurted out what had happened as he hastened to fulfill his master's errand.

The news was as startling as had been the bombardment at dawn a week ago, and even more incredible. They stared amazedly from the man on the bed to the woman who had volunteered to nurse him; the woman in the linsey-woolsey olive-green dress, with the firm chin and the large, capable hands; the woman who that morning had been a lowly servant and now had suddenly become a duchess. From this moment on they would be expected to curtsy to her! The Duke had played a scurvy trick on them.

Defensively, George put his arm about Nancy's shoulder. "Congratulations, your Grace."

"Stop your nonsense," she said, even now not fully realizing what had happened. "Please, good sirs and ladies, his Grace has had more excitement than is good for him. You can see that he's in pain. He must have quiet. Please go."

"Let them stay," commanded the man on the bed. "I want plenty of witnesses to my will."

Stunned, they stood there, not knowing what to say or do.

The lawyer arrived, puffing with exertion. George, following the Duke's dictation and the wording of the attorney, wrote down the fact that William James Henry Tamerskey, Duke of Thewes, being close to death but of some mind, herein bequeathed all his property, real and personal, to his devoted wife. When it was over, the Duke ordered them out of the room. Stunned, they obeyed.

Nancy caught Hal by the hand. "Am I really a duchess?" she asked plaintively.

"So you are," growled the Duke before Hal could reply. "I've made you a duchess and I've made you rich. I'm not sure that I've made you happy."

"But, sir, you shouldn't have done it. I was content as I was—oh, quite, sir! I never yearned for wealth. I——"

"Stop chattering. Bring me a glass of water."

"Y-yes, sir." As she poured the liquid from a pitcher on the table her hands trembled so that she spilled some of it. "Here you are, and never fear. I'll not hold you to the marriage, sir. Just rest now. Just rest."

"Not a cent must you give to my brother or his family, you understand?" After drinking the water which she held to his lips, he began to chuckle. "How surprised he'll be when he knows I've outwitted him. He—" He dropped into sudden sleep, smiling, as though relishing the thought of what he had done.

The Queen was incensed that the Duke had dared to marry without her consent, which she would never have given. The ladies of the court, once they had recovered from their astonishment, accused the Duke of being a traitor to his class, and agreed that they would snub the new Duchess. Nancy seemed unaware of their antagonism. Her whole attention was given to her patient.

Three days later she was a widow, and since it was impossible to take the body to the Duke's family estates, he was given a quiet funeral in Burlington. The Queen, to emphasize her displeasure, did not attend.

When the erstwhile Mrs. Cheam, solemn and dazed, returned to the room where her husband had died, she was accompanied only by Hal and George.

"You must be very tired," said Hal softly.

Her Grace seemed not to be listening. Weakly, she sank into a chair. "Me—a duchess!" she muttered.

"And one of the richest women in Europe," said Hal, smiling, for it seemed laughable, like some sort of charade.

"Do I have castles and everything?"

"You have a fine town house in London; you have a gorgeous place at Budleigh Salterton overlooking the sea; and another mammoth estate at Crewe, your Grace."

"Neither castles nor wealth mean happiness," Nancy answered, no longer dazed but accepting the situation with characteristic good sense. "Well, I suppose I shall get used to it, get used to people curtsying and calling me 'your Grace' and all. Fortunately I've been around the Wades so much that I know about court etiquette. I'm not apt to make a fool of myself."

"You can't serve as my maid any more," Hal told her. She sighed. "No, I suppose not. I must write to Jerry at once. Oh, won't he be surprised! I've no idea where he is, but I guess I can reach him through Mr. Milton. God grant nothing has happened to the lad. I'll get some writing paper and——"

"No," George said firmly, "you'll send for it. No longer must you wait on yourself, you know. You'll have to get several personal maids. You already have the Duke's four servants he brought with him. You must get yourself some new clothes and you must make your formal bow to the Queen. Hal and I are here to help you in any way we can."

"Goodness! It's like the Bible says—'In the twinkling of an eye all will be changed.' And what did I do for the poor man except what I'd do for any sick creature? I'm a duchess. What does that make my Jerry?"

"Heir to a great fortune," replied George.

"Poor boy. He was brought up to work for every farthing, to save every penny."

"He'll have plenty to do," George told her, "managing those estates of yours. And speaking of estates, as soon as possible you must visit them, get to know them and your servants. You had better leave as soon as possible."

"Leave you?" she looked at Hal. "Who'll look after you?"

"Never mind about that," said George. "The Duke's servants will escort you. They'll get the horses you need and you had better be off. I'm sure that her Majesty won't try to detain you."

"That she won't! You'll promise to come and see me, both of you? And stay as long as you can? Why, you're my family! You've a home with me forever if you like." She looked at Hal. "Oh, and by the way, your ladyship, that bag of gold you gave me. You must take it back. I—I won't be needing it—now."

8 ✿

the fateful meeting

DURING THAT STAY AT BOYNTON HALL THE QUEEN WAS NOT idle. The death of the Duke left her untouched. She had more important things to think about. Men from the surrounding counties came in droves to pledge their allegiance to her and join her forces. She received them graciously, distributing among them some of the weapons she had brought. In the midst of this she found time to receive the new Duchess, who asked permission to leave and look after her estates. Mary's manner was haughty as she agreed that this was wise.

"*Tiens!* That such a woman should be elevated to the peerage!" she exclaimed when the Duchess had backed out of the room.

As for her ladies, they remained furious, considering that the Duke must have been mad to elevate "that woman" to their ranks.

"I know how they feel," said the Duchess mildly just before leaving, "but they needn't resent having to curtsy to me. I've no intention of becoming a fixture at court.

I'm a country woman and I'd be happy enough back in my wee cottage at Shottery."

"You're every bit as good as the best of us," answered Hal. "And don't let the fact that you own a few castles intimidate you. You'll know how to manage them, for you managed Langdon Hall. Oh, Ch— er—your Grace, I hate saying good-by to you!"

"Stop calling me 'your Grace.' And since I'm not Mrs. Cheam any more, maybe you'd better just call me Nancy. Oh, I'd like to see my Jerry's face when he gets my letter! If only I knew where he was! I've decided to go to Budleigh Salterton and wait there until I hear from him. If you need me, there's where I'll be. Well, so the time's come for us to part. Now don't worry about me, dear. I'll be escorted by the Duke's men and if we run into any Cavaliers I am the Duchess of Thewes, while if we meet any Roundheads my name's Nancy Cheam. Remember now, my home is yours—yours and your family's. I shall be lonesome for you."

They parted affectionately, Hal and George promising to come to Budleigh Salterton as soon as they could. As Hal stood watching the new Duchess ride off, her mind was not focused upon that departing matronly figure but on Jerry. Where was he? Hurt, perhaps? Or lying dead in some battle-field? The longing to see him, to know how he was, was like a perpetual ache, making her restless and silent, and she was glad when just a week after the departure of the Duchess, an escort of two thousand more Cavaliers arrived from York for the Queen. They were headed by the Marquess of Montrose, and to the delight of Hal and George, the Marquess of Langdon was his second in command.

Life in camp had done nothing to change the Marquess.

He was as rotund, as ruddy and jolly as ever, though his hair had more gray in it.

"You were a fool to suggest breaking the marriage contract," he said when Hal had told him the news, "and a naughty girl to do it without my permission. Odds fish, Hal, we could use that money now! Of course, if the King wins, all of us who have contributed to his victory will be handsomely rewarded, but meanwhile the Wades can well envy that proverbial church mouse."

"If he wins? Father, have you any doubt of that?"

"Frankly, yes—although I wouldn't say so to anyone else. We have fought well. Prince Rupert is a great fighter. The King is a brave leader. We're all vastly encouraged by the coming of the Queen with this ammunition. On the other hand, the army of Lord Essex has been freshly equipped. Though ordered to advance upon Oxford, instead he recaptures Reading and now his forces remain idle around Brill. They say his ranks have been thinned by disease. Of course, there are pockets of Roundheads everywhere."

"I wonder if Jerry is with them? Father, when I remember what we owe to Jerry . . . !" She told him about the night the Roundheads burst into her room and about the long trip to Felixstone.

"Yes," he admitted, "we're much indebted to that boy. Hmm. Heir to a great fortune now. Once when he said he'd repay me the money I'd spent for his education, I laughed. But I need that money now. Odds fish, Hal, how am I going to rebuild Langdon Hall? On the money due from the tenants? Hardly. Hmm. Now I wonder——"

"You wonder what, sir?"

"When the war's over—and how can it possibly last six months longer?—I shall contact Cheam—er—the Duchess. It may be that I can arrange a plight-troth——"

"Oh, Father! I don't want you to arrange anything!"

"Why not? You'd better catch that boy before someone else gets the same idea. All at once he's one of the most eligible young men in England!"

Now that sufficient escort had arrived, Mary and her party left Burlington. Her Majesty had but one idea—to meet Charles as soon as possible and deliver the munitions he so sorely needed. When her ladies suggested that they were fatigued she insisted upon taking no time for rest, and moved on at increased speed.

She was gay and tireless as she rode on horseback at the head of her troops, crossing the wolds toward Malton, well guarded with six pieces of cannon, two large mortars, and two hundred and fifty wagons loaded with arms, ammunition, money and baggage.

In every town she passed through, she gathered recruits until her force swelled to gratifying proportions. The men were filled with admiration for this slender, delicately-made woman who, with her ladies, rode through rain and wind and sun, and ate her meals on the field. Having left garrisons at Malton and Stamford Bridge, the troops reached York in March, and she agreed to rest there for several days.

"Hal," she cried delightedly, her eyes glowing, "the war will soon end! I am like a she-general riding at the head of my troops, *non?*"

"God for Queen Mary!" replied Hal. "Is it true, what I heard, madam—that Parliament is trying to make peace with the King?"

"*Oui, c'est vrai.* But he must not! I sent him a letter. I said he must not! *Jamais!*"

"But your Majesty wants peace?"

"*Certainement.* But first Parliament must be disbanded.

126

He must not capitulate now! Hull is ours. All Yorkshire is ours. *Voilà!*"

A few days later, in early April, the Queen's army was on the march again, hastening toward Oxford, its leader looking fresh and young, confident of victory, though she knew that between her and Charles stood the Parliamentary forces under Lords Essex and Fairfax, determined to keep those two apart and thus prevent the King from receiving such formidable reinforcement. They feared to attack the Queen's forces, which were growing larger day by day as Mary, an entrancing and inspiring sight on her superb horse, continued to attract recruits.

Strong as they were, they wished to avoid conflict with the enemy, and they had to move at a wearisome pace, so slowly that the journey to Oxford required six months.

The ladies were nerve-wracked, weary and worn, but Mary, her spirits still high, seemed to be sustained by a power beyond her frail body. Her officers stood the journey well.

Being Cavaliers, they were sportsmen, and a pause meant time for backgammon, dicing, archery, quoits and hawking. None of them seemed worried, and all had voracious appetites. Food, supplied by the farmers, was plentiful, and camp was fragrant with the odors of chicken, plovers, woodcock and quail turning on dozens of spits. Services on Sunday were unfailing, the Queen and her Catholic followers at one end of the broad field, the Episcopalians on the opposite side. In the evenings there would be male voices harmonizing in rollicking Cavalier songs.

The farmers watched them solemnly as they passed, and then returned to their fields to sow their barley, oats, corn and vegetables. Anvils worked overtime furnishing implements of war for one side or the other.

Slow, cautious, alert, the Queen's army moved on through Goole, Scunthorpe, Gainsborough, Tuxford and finally Newark where in late June they were forced to pause for a brief rest. Around Oxford and in the mid-counties the King and Prince Rupert fought and skirmished, intent upon clearing the way for the royal lovers to meet.

The nearer she came to Oxford the more vibrant became Queen Mary. The long marches had had no effect whatever. Scouts were sent in all directions to locate enemy positions. There were reports that the enemy was at Nottingham, Leicester, Derby, planning to intercept her. Mary, whom her forces proudly called the Generalissima, remained radiant and undaunted. With three thousand foot soldiers and thirty companies of horse and dragoons, she had the feeling of being invincible.

As she rode along, never far from the Queen, Hal's thoughts constantly reverted to Jerry. If only she knew that he was well! She was tempted to write to John Milton for information, but how could she use a Royalist messenger to penetrate Cambridge, a Puritan stronghold?

It was late June before Mary received word that the King's forces had finally cleared the way and it was now comparatively safe for her to proceed.

"God for Queen Mary!" cried the men as they left Newark on the third of July. Four days later they had reached Ashby and from there they proceeded to Wassal. On the tenth they reached King's Norton and the next day they were on the Wades' home grounds at Stratford where they were greeted with shouts of welcome by the King's army under Prince Rupert, the King's handsome nephew, son of his sister Elizabeth.

On the following day the greatly augmented army went through Shottery and passed the gaunt ruins of Langdon

Hall. Hal's eyes filled with tears, and to avoid looking at it she turned her head away.

"*Qu'avez-vous?*" asked the Queen lightly.

"That was my home and I loved it."

Mary shrugged. "*N'import.* One day I shall build you a better one. Ah, Hal, soon I shall see him! So long we have been separated! Almost two years, *non?* Someday you will know how sad it is not to be with the man you love."

"Do you think you're the only woman in the world who knows how sad it is?" thought Hal. At least the Queen knew that her loved one was alive and well and was coming to greet her, his heart pounding with anticipation.

It was in the Vale of Keinton that Charles and Mary finally met. Looking on at that meeting, so touching in its tenderness, many of the most hardened soldiers were unashamed of the tears that welled up in their eyes. Mary and Charles were a splendid-looking couple. No one ever sat a horse more beautifully than did Charles I. He was a tall, well-built man with waving hair that reached to his flat, lace-edged collar. He was lean and regal, with a nose a trifle too large, and a pointed chin beard and mustache. With his straight shoulders and proud bearing, he looked every inch a king. That day, as always, he was richly and impeccably attired.

Beside him his wife looked smaller than ever, her oval face fairly aglow with joy.

When the King, relaxed and smiling, had greeted his subjects, everyone was in hilarious spirits. The whole town rejoiced in the wonderful accomplishment of the Queen, and suddenly the travelers no longer felt jaded and taut. Everyone seemed miraculously revived and all shared the Queen's own elation.

Hal had always felt a special fondness for Oxford, with

its graceful spires golden in the setting sun and that dreamy, wistful softness that came at twilight, a kind of sweet and solemn magic that she was sure could be found nowhere else in the world. On Sundays it was a pleasant thing to awaken to the kindly, cheery sound of the bells of Christ Church.

Oxford meant rest. It meant getting out one's best clothes again. It meant banquets and dancing, for Oxford was now the seat of the court, the place where one found luxury, gaiety, graciousness and refinement. All the ladies seemed to blossom anew, for they had been reunited with their husbands and sweethearts. All except Hal.

"Father," she said pensively as they were walking away from Christ Church one Sabbath morning, "can't we go and visit Cheam—er—Nancy? I had a letter from her yesterday. She's at Budleigh Salterton. She insists that we regard her homes as ours. She's lonely. She begs me to come. She hasn't heard from Jerry and she's terribly afraid that he is—dead. Can't we go? Wouldn't their Majesties give us leave? We've been in Oxford all winter now and——"

"I'm afraid not, Hal. It's a matter of duty. And speaking of duty, you'll have to hurry or you'll be late for your service to the Queen."

For the past two weeks Mary had been unlike herself. Members of her court had never seen her like this, lethargic, weak and fretful. The doctor had said that this was not caused by the fact that she was bearing another child, and he was puzzled. The King was anxious.

As Hal entered the Queen's apartment Charles and the physician were just leaving. Hal knelt before the monarch, but he passed by without even seeing her.

"Rheumatic fever, sire," Dr. Mayerne was saying, "no

doubt brought on by the hardships she endured last spring during that long, hard march."

"But there must be something you can do to save her!" Charles insisted urgently.

"She might find relief from her pain by bathing in the springs at Bath. This is the only hope. As yet there is no remedy for . . ."

They walked out of the room.

The outer room was filled with ladies. "She's worse," said the Countess of Carlyle. "She's in terrible pain. Both Dr. Mayerne and Dr. Lister prescribe the springs of Bath, but it's said that Bath's in the hands of the enemy. The King has sent spies to make sure. Go in to her, Hal. She's been asking for you."

As Hal entered the bedchamber and knelt, she found Mary in bed moaning and writhing.

"Hal . . . Hal. *Vous voilà.* I cannot endure this pain. I must get to Bath or I shall die. . . . *Ouvrez la fenêtre.*"

Hal opened the window and took a chair beside the bed. Mary looked pale, and in the one day since Hal had seen her, her eyes seemed to have sunk deeper into their sockets.

"Madam, how can you go to Bath? The place is said to be occupied by the Roundheads. Besides, you might not stand the trip. Come, perhaps massage might help. Have I your Majesty's permission?"

But not medicine, massage, hot bricks or cold compresses alleviated the Queen's pain. She grew steadily worse. She was obsessed with the conviction that only the springs at Bath would benefit her and she grew childish in her fretful insistence that she must go there.

What to do? To let her go seemed the equivalent of letting her commit suicide. Never had Charles been so troubled. Not only did he adore his wife, but she had been his adviser. When he would have given in, she had stood firm, goading him to resist, to keep on fighting. Now she herself was fighting for her very life.

"I must get away from here!" Mary kept saying. "If I am to live, I must get to the springs. Let us go. It is soon dark. We must start. Tell them to pack. Hal, *venez avec moi!*"

"Yes, madam, I will go with you, but we can't leave quite yet. Next week, perhaps."

"Now! Today! *Je suis malade. Je n'en puis plus.* We shall run away, you and I."

Hal realized that it was impossible for her to ask to be relieved from her duties now, and she wrote as much to Nancy. Perhaps Mary was right. Perhaps her sole chance of recovery lay in those mineral springs at Bath, which had been known for their health-giving qualities even back in the ancient Roman days.

Bath, on the Avon, was a long and perilous journey from Oxford, especially for a woman in Mary's condition, and Charles still hesitated when his spies returned saying that the town was no longer occupied, though pockets of Roundheads were everywhere in its vicinity.

But his wife's condition failed to improve; rather, it worsened. What was equally alarming, Oxford itself was now no longer safe. The Parliamentary forces were approaching and a battle for the city seemed inevitable. Much as he dreaded parting from the woman he adored, Charles had no choice now but to send her away.

The ladies attendant upon the Queen began to pack. There were only seven of them now. The others, terrified at the prospect of that trip to Bath, had made feverish excuses and scattered off. Only a handful of officers could

132

serve the Queen as escort, for it was necessary that they travel as secretly as possible, making no royal display.

George was among those chosen to go, as was Jeffrey Hudson, who pleaded to be allowed to remain at her Majesty's side. At dawn one morning they placed the Queen, her body wasted away almost to a skeleton, in a wagon lined with feather mattresses and pillows. Charles, miserable at the thought of another parting, rode with his wife as far as Abingdon. Neither could restrain their tears as they said farewell on that chill, misty morning.

The courtiers who accompanied the Queen were amazed when they met with no trouble on the way to Bath, but Mary's illness did not abate on the way, and it grew worse when they told her of the King's losses at the Battle of Newbury.

Arriving at Bath, they found to their dismay that they could not remain. War had been there, devastating and cruel. Houses were demolished. The streets were full of corpses lying in a state of decay. And what was worse, pestilence had broken out. They had to go somewhere else at once. Where? Exeter was known to be loyal. They must go there. But by what route? There were pockets of Roundheads everywhere in this neighborhood. Any move was hazardous. Danger lurked on every road.

One day, weary of the stench of death and the weeping attendants, disturbed by the Queen's piteous moans and the peril that was everywhere, Hal decided to take a walk, hoping to find some quiet spot on the river. Tensely and hurriedly she moved through the filthy streets until she was outside the town where the air was clean. When she reached the riverbank, her thoughts, as they always did, turned longingly to Jerry. Concern for his safety was uppermost.

She wondered if he knew of the change in the fortunes of his grandmother, and if he had found some girl who attracted him. How long it had been since she had seen him! It had been almost two years since they had parted on the dock at Felixstone. . . .

Finding herself walking among waist-high rushes with no house in sight, and no sign of life, she suddenly paused, alarmed, for it seemed that the motion of those rushes denoted the presence of someone besides herself. She listened. Yes, there it was again, a slight rustle. Terrified, she turned to flee when a masculine voice whispered, "Don't scream!"

"Who—who———"

Then, directly in front of her, he popped up from the rushes, his shirt torn and soiled, his hair ruffled by the wind. For an instant she doubted that she was really seeing him. He had been so strongly in her mind that she thought this must be an apparition.

Taking her hand, he pulled her down into the rushes where they could be hidden.

"Hal—" Jerry murmured. "Oh, my darling, my sweet!"

9 ✿

the big decision

ACCORDING TO CUSTOM NO "LADY" WAS PERMITTED TO BE alone with any man not of her immediate family; no "lady" allowed herself to be kissed except by her husband; no "lady" confessed her love until after a man had placed a wedding ring on her finger. But here was Lady Henrietta Wade hidden by the rushes, in the arms of a lithe, tattered Roundhead, permitting herself to be kissed, and actually clinging to him!

"Jerry! Oh, Jerry, I've been so worried about you! Are you all right, darling? Oh, Jerry, I love you. I love you so!"

"And I love you, more than my life."

Then, abruptly, decorum returned to both of them. They drew apart, though he reached for her hand, holding it tenderly.

"I'm sorry," he murmured. "I shouldn't have done that. I shouldn't have kissed you. I apologize."

"No, no, no. I wanted you to! I've wanted you to for a long time. Oh, it's wonderful to see you, Jerry, to know you're all right, to know that you love me. But how in the world did you——"

"I knew you were in Bath. I've been watching you ever since you came, hoping for a chance to talk to you. Oh, Hal—I mean, my lady—I've no right to say that I love you, but I can't get you out of my mind. I've tried."

"Jerry, I——"

"I've fought this love as though it were an enemy. But the truth is, I'm lost without you, dearest. And now here you are. For a little while we're together—such a little while!" He gazed at her adoringly. "How beautiful you are—more beautiful than ever. Your hair—it's growing out again. Oh, just being with you, just looking at you—" he broke off, glancing about apprehensively. "We won't be able to talk long. You shouldn't have come out alone like this. Promise me you won't do it again. Stay close to your people."

"Jerry, what are you doing here?"

"The whole district is honeycombed with our contingents. We've small camps all through here. I and several others were delegated to spy on the movements of the Queen. Is she really ill or is this a trick?"

"No, she's seriously ill, and besides, she's about to have a child. It's expected any day. She came to Bath hoping that the springs would help her, but——"

"You know, of course, that if we get hold of her she'll be put in the Tower and quickly executed on the charge of high treason."

"Yes. We know." She noticed that he wore no uniform. The only indication that he belonged to Essex's forces was the army scarf around his neck. She smiled fondly. "You are my enemy. How can I love you so?"

"Dearest, you're in danger and there's little I can do to protect you. Vigilant as we are, we didn't know of the Queen's coming to Bath until she arrived. But now she's watched. We know she can't stay in Bath long, but every road and byway out of it is patrolled. Why is her company so small? They couldn't protect her against us!"

"It was thought wise. The idea was not to attract attention. Oh, Jerry, what shall we do? Where can we go? Our intention is to go to Exeter which, we hear, is still Royalist."

"It won't be Royalist for long," he replied grimly. "But yes, for the present you could go there."

"But how? We know the roads are infested with Roundheads, just waiting to pounce on us the minute we leave Bath. We're trapped."

"No. There's a way. Listen carefully. I'll tell you the roads you must avoid, the ones we are watching—the only roads leading in any direction."

"Why tell me of them? If they're the only roads, then we're certain to be caught."

"No. I've scouted this whole territory. There's a way. There's an old path, never used now. It leads to Exeter. Before the new roads were made in Queen Elizabeth's time, the farmers used this one to take their pigs and cattle to the Exeter market; but now it's abandoned. The Roundheads will ignore it, believing that none of the Queen's party could possibly know about it. Once on it, though, you must move swiftly and quietly." He told her how the little-known path was to be reached. "Now," he asked when explicit directions had been given, "do you have that clearly in mind? Oh, Hal, if anything should happen to you——"

"Thanks for telling me about this way of escape. Is there anything else we should know?"

"Only this. You won't be able to stay in Exeter long. In about a week—ten days—we're planning to put it under a state of siege. Be sure of this—I shall watch you as much as I can, but that probably won't be much, especially after you leave Bath, though I'll try to get the job of spying in Exeter. Oh, Hal, my dearest, if only I had words to tell you what's in my heart!"

"Sometime you will—when this dreadful war ends. Wars can't go on forever. When it's over we must find each other. I'm sure that God has ordained it. Let us agree to meet at Budleigh Salterton."

"Why there?"

"Why, didn't you know? About your grandmother?"

"Grandmother! I noticed that she wasn't with you. Has she gone back to Shottery? Is she well?"

He listened incredulously while she told him what had happened to Nancy and how, shortly before leaving Oxford she had had a letter from her telling her whereabouts.

"This is the most fantastic thing I've ever heard of!" he exclaimed when she had finished. "Incredible!"

"She wrote you about it, sending the letter in care of Mr. Milton."

"We've been moving about so fast . . . Besides, messengers are often killed or taken prisoner. No, I never got the letter. I wrote to her, thinking she was with you at Oxford, but—ssh! Stoop lower!"

She could see two young Roundheads coming toward them, searching for something in the rushes.

"They're looking for bodies, to bury them," Jerry whispered. "Since the plague the townspeople too weak to bury the corpses have a way of tossing them in the rushes."

He waited, hoping that the men would turn in the opposite direction, but they kept coming toward them, beating the rushes with long pikes.

"Stay here," whispered Jerry, "until I can get them away, then hurry back to Bath!"

Not a moment too soon he sprang up, facing his comrades merrily.

"Ho, there! Are you trying to run me through?"

"Jerry! You're a fine one, popping up like a jack-in-the-box. Scared us half to death!"

He walked toward them nonchalantly. "Nothing to be found in this direction." He flung his arms about their shoulders. "Come on, let's get back to camp." He succeeded in turning them about so that their backs were to Hal.

When they were at a safe distance she rose and raced back to the inn, hurrying up the stairs to George's room where she found him lying on the bed, his valet polishing his boots. He sat up at her entrance.

"Hal! Don't you ever knock? Wh— have you seen a ghost?"

She turned to the servant. "Finish that outside, Swaim."

The man picked up the boots, rags and grease and went into the hall. Hal closed the door behind him and spoke in an excited whisper.

"I've just seen Jerry!"

"Our Jerry? Here?"

"We must leave for Exeter as soon as possible." Breathlessly, she told him about the back road.

"Blessings on our friend the Roundhead!" he exclaimed, hurriedly donning his doublet. "What? Do I detect a blush?"

"I love him, George, and if you jest about it, I'll——"

"Oh, a little teasing never hurt anyone, but seriously, as heir to the Duchess of Thewes our Jerry's an excellent match. I suppose you thought of that, you minx. But we'll

139

discuss that later." He walked to the door and opened it. "Swaim, bring me those boots. Never mind whether they're polished or not. Put them on me and don't be slow about it. Hal, we must go at once to the Queen."

Mary was in bed, but she was neither moaning nor twitching. The despair she was enduring acted as an opiate, lessening the terrible pain in her legs. She was deathly pale, her cheeks sunken, her hair dull and disordered.

"La," she moaned, "where have you been? The child will be born soon. I know it."

"Nevertheless, your Majesty," said George, forgetting to kneel, "we must leave at once. Tonight if possible. Hal, tell her what you have told me."

"Your Majesty, you remember I told you once about—about a Roundhead I was in love with? You said it was merely foolishness and I'd get over it. Well, I haven't gotten over it, though it has been a long time since I've seen him. But today I went for a walk outside the town along the river, and I saw him, and this is what he told me. . . ."

Mary listened intently while Hal repeated what Jerry had said about the vigilance of the Roundheads, the roads and the unknown path.

"*Oui.* We should leave at once. But this man, you are sure he is to be trusted?"

"I have trusted him with my heart, madam, and someday, please God, I shall marry him."

"*À la bonne heure!* We will trust him. Summon the others. Hal, help me to sit up. Ah, *mon Dieu*, how can I I go to Exeter when it hurts so to move even such a little bit? God help me!"

An hour later when the room was filled with her attendants, Mary spoke firmly, giving her orders with the crispness of a commander.

"But, madam," said the Countess of Carlyle, quivering with fear, "how can you do it? It will kill you!"

"I will do it. *Il me faut le faire.* First, I must send a letter to the King, telling him where I am going. Lady Cicely, bring me writing paper and pen. Get a messenger. Be ready, all of you, to leave just before dawn."

Just before daylight, while Bath was still sleeping, they carried the Queen to the wagon and followed that barely discernible, winding path uphill and downhill. Finally, on May 3, without incident, they reached Exeter, where the Queen and her party were received at Bedford House. Not expecting them, the hostess, a middle-aged woman named Lady Morton, was flustered and frightened. Humbly she apologized because accommodations would not be what they would have found in happier times, but the Queen wearily brushed that aside. Despite the discomfort of the trip, the emergency of the situation seemed to have given her new strength.

It was quiet at Bedford House and the air was clean. Mary was put to bed at once and Lady Morton sent her servants scampering in search of more food, which was scarce in Exeter.

Near the end of the month they were surprised at the arrival of the King's physician, Sir Theodore Mayerne, who had brought with him Sir Martin Lister. Mayerne actually disliked the Queen, being convinced that she, and not the King, was responsible for the present conflict. But he was devoted to Charles and had started posthaste from London after receiving a brief note, *Mayerne: For the love of* me, *go to my wife!*

The siege had begun and the noise was deafening when, on June 16, the Queen gave birth to a girl. Two days later the doctors left.

Ten days after their departure the siege became so intensified that the commander of the town sent word to her Majesty that he must surrender. The Queen called all her people to her bedside. She seemed stronger and there was a faint flush on her thin cheeks, but her lips were colorless and her usually flashing eyes were devoid of luster.

"Pay attention, my friends. What are we to do? *Je ne sais pas.* But we cannot remain here. It is only a question of a day before the Roundheads take this place. It is unwise for us to return to Bath, *non?* What do you think? I am at my wit's end."

"We couldn't possibly get to Bath without passing through enemy lines," said George.

Several of the men nodded. There was a slight, thoughtful pause.

"The back road we took before?"

"The Roundheads are watching every move your Majesty makes," said Hal. "The country from here to Bath is overrun with them now. Even that back road is no longer safe. This morning as I ventured on an errand for her Majesty I heard some men saying that."

"But we must get out of Exeter!" insisted Mary. "This town will fall to the Roundheads any moment. One thing I can do—write to Lord Essex and ask his permission to go to Bath for my health."

They were silent, afraid to advise.

"We-ell," said George gravely, "it couldn't do any harm but I doubt that it will do any good."

So Mary wrote to the Parliamentary general and George agreed to carry the message. He returned promptly with a note from Essex which filled the whole company with dismay.

Madam:
   It is my intention to escort your Majesty to London where your presence is required to answer to Parliament for having levied war upon England.

"That settles that," said George dryly.

"It means only one thing. He will take me to London as a prisoner."

"No!" cried Hal. "He shan't!"

"We'll die before that happens," cried the dwarf.

Several of the women began to weep. The Duke of Hurley paced back and forth.

"If only we hadn't left Oxford!" said the Countess.

"If only we could get back there!" put in the dwarf.

"Let us be calm," advised one of the priests.

The Countess seemed to resent this. "Calm! How can you talk of being calm when the city is about to be surrendered to these despicable Roundheads?"

"It will do no good to get excited," said the Queen in a low voice, but her thin hands trembled and her eyes were bleak with despair. "Sit down, your Grace."

Commanded to do so, the Duke obeyed. He sat on a straight-backed chair, his knees twitching.

Hudson said something, but a sudden burst of cannon drowned out his words. He wiped the perspiration from his forehead with a lace-edged handkerchief.

"This is the time to pray," said the other priest.

"Pray!" exclaimed the Duke. "This is the time for action! Think of something! Can't any of you think of something? Shall we stay here and fight?" he gave a short, contemptuous laugh. "Ha! What fools we'd be to think we could gain anything by that? So few of us!"

"It must be that there is something we can do!" insisted Mary.

"We're trapped. We're lost," sobbed one of the women. "Why try to do anything? Why not just accept our fate? Our situation is hopeless."

"Utterly hopeless," wailed another.

"Stop talking like that!" said Hal, with characteristic verve.

"So few you are," replied Mary ruefully. "No, no, he shall not arrest me. We must find some way to escape. Courage! There must be a way."

"Could we—could we get out of Exeter disguised?" asked Hal. "This house is certainly being watched, but if we could disguise ourselves and leave after dark in small groups? Two or three at a time? They would think we're only Lady Morton's servants. No one would pay any attention to us."

They considered this lengthily. At last, in a tone of decision, Mary broke the uneasy silence.

"Mais certainement. A good idea. It is the only way. We will go as soon as we can. Lady Morton, I must leave my child with you. I know you will take good care of her. To bring her with me—that is impossible."

"I'll do my best to care for the Princess, madam," promised Lady Morton feelingly.

"To leave my baby—it is a sad thing. But it must be done. Hurry! Hurry now. Find us clothes to disguise ourselves in. Wait! We do not go to Bath. Better we go to Plymouth."

"Yes," said the dwarf. "Plymouth's a royal garrison; besides, it's on the sea—in case your Majesty might want to escape from England."

"*Vous avez raison,* my little man. We will go to Plymouth. Quick, my friends. Fetch the disguises."

"Your Majesty can't leave this house alone," said Hal. "Whom do you choose to be with you?"

"One of my priests, my Lord George and you. George is young and strong and I will need his support. So it is settled. All of you, *prenez garde!*"

"I know this district well," spoke up Lady Morton, "especially the way to Plymouth. In a wood between here and there—off from it slightly and hidden by a grove of trees—there's a hut. It has been vacant for a long time. Your Majesty could use that as a rendezvous for your party."

"Good!" cried Mary, her pain forgotten. "We shall meet in the hut between here and Plymouth. *Me comprenez-vous?* We will go disguised. We will travel by twos and threes. We meet at the hut. Is it far? No matter. We shall keep our going a secret so that the Roundheads will believe we are still in Exeter!"

Lady Morton's serving people were loyal and when they were called upon to donate their clothes they responded willingly. Styles worn by lower servants, those not required to wear livery, had been unchanged for years. Women wore dark, practical dresses with white petticoats, full skirts reaching to the ankles, long aprons gathered at the waist, and sometimes a white kerchief around the neck, a shawl or a cape.

The Queen's ladies and gentlemen had to leave their lavish wardrobes, but the skirts and aprons provided for them had large pockets into which they stuffed their jewels. Small bundles were also permissible for both men and women.

Mary's dress was dark blue, and she pushed her black, tightly curled hair under a white cap. Hal's dress was dark brown, of a heavy hand-woven wool, and her hair was now long enough to be tied back from her face with a yellow ribbon. Their shoes were sturdy, with low heels.

"How can people walk in shoes like this?" asked Mary, but she did not complain.

Henrietta Maria, Princess of France, Queen of England, was the daughter of a brave king, the sister of a king and the wife of a king, and she proved her mettle now as, dry-eyed, she bade good-by to her attendants, all as drably garbed as herself. Leaving her tiny daughter was not easy, but she stifled her tears, and accompanied only by Hal, George and the priest, who was disguised as a peasant, she left Bedford House by the servants' entrance.

It was now dark and the spring night was overcast. They did not dare risk carrying a torch. At first Mary walked firmly, but her weakness increased as she continued, moving unnoticed through the streets toward the city gate while shots landed on all sides.

"The gate—is it much farther?" she asked pathetically, stifling her moans.

"About three miles," answered George. "If your Majesty will permit me?"

"*Oui.* I—I feel that I must fall. Hold me up."

He put his arm about her tiny waist, half carrying her.

"We must find a place for her Majesty to rest," said the priest in a worried tone. "Many people, trying to escape the siege, have abandoned their homes. There must be a place where we can take her. It's still early evening. Candles are lit. If we come to a house that's dark, let us stop there."

"*Merci,*" muttered Mary.

Eyes alert for a darkened house, they kept walking until finally they found a shack with its single window darkened, its door opening flush with the street. While George supported the now half-fainting Queen, the priest knocked at the door. Receiving no reply, he opened it.

The place consisted of one room, empty except for some straw in one corner. A rat scampered away as the four people entered. George deposited the Queen on the straw and then closed the door, which had no lock.

"We wouldn't dare light a light even if we had one," said the priest. "God has surely led us to this place."

"I suppose we can hide here for a while," said George as he and the priest sank to the dusty floor, using the wall as a brace for their backs.

Hal stooped above the Queen. "Your Majesty, how do you feel?" She knew it was a foolish question, but she could think of nothing else to say.

"Not too well," answered Mary. "We shall stay here— just a little while. Then we must go on. I am sorry I make so much trouble for you. *Apportez-moi un verre d'eau fraîche, s'il vous plaît.*"

"Your Majesty, there is no water."

"*Ça va.* I am . . ." She drifted into sleep and Hal sank to the floor beside her.

"I'm thirsty, too," she said. "There must be water somewhere."

"If there is," replied her brother drearily, "I wouldn't know where to find it. In the daylight I can probably look for a well in the back yard, but now I suggest that we get what sleep we can."

They had to remain in the shack for the next two days, since it was plainly impossible to move the Queen. Besides, the Roundheads had now entered the city, clashing in hand-to-hand combat with the citizens. Hunger tore at the foursome in the shack, though they were spared the agony of thirst, for at dawn the first morning George had ventured into the small back yard where he found a well, and not far from it, a rusty pail.

The refugees scarcely dared to whisper, for dozens of times Roundhead soldiers passed the door, sometimes even pausing near the window.

"By heaven," they heard one of them say, "we'll carry the head of Mary to London. Parliament will give us a reward of fifty thousand crowns for it!"

"Where the devil is she?" replied his companion. "We've searched Bedford House. How could she get away? She must be in this town somewhere."

They walked on. "How they hate me!" Mary murmured. "Hal—George—we must get out of here! I am stronger now."

"We can't," answered George. "The fighting's still going on. Besides, I'm so weak from lack of food and sleep, I doubt if we could get far. This floor gets harder by the minute."

"We'll starve if we stay here," whispered Hal, "and we'll be killed if we leave."

"I am praying," said the priest. "God will deliver us. Have faith. He knows where we are."

"What's stopping Him, then?" asked George bitterly. "He's had two days! Why doesn't He do something?"

Mary was fingering her rosary, but her eyes were on the door. Every hour seemed an eternity. As twilight came, followed by pitch darkness, they were like drugged people. Then suddenly the door, which had no lock, was thrust open and a tall man entered carrying a torch. The Queen gasped.

They could not see the man's face, for the abrupt glare of the torch had almost blinded them. He walked a few feet inside the room so that the torch could illumine the entire area.

"Thank God I've found you!" he said in a voice that was almost a whisper. "I've been looking for you everywhere!"

"*Mon Dieu!*" gasped Mary.

But Hal had recognized the voice. "Jerry!" she cried. "Don't be afraid, your Majesty. It's Jerry Vane!"

He spoke quickly in clipped, carefully muffled tones. "You must get out of here. Where are you going?"

"Plymouth," answered George.

"By dawn the road there will be cleared. It will be safe for you to leave then. The fighting is moving to the opposite end of Exeter. Take the road to the right after you get outside the gate. If I find any members of your party before then I'll send them to you. Here." He tossed something into the room.

Almost before it hit the floor he turned away and went out, closing the door. They heard him as he spoke to several fellow-soldiers who could not have been far behind him when he opened the door.

"No one in there but an old woman. Her family has deserted her. She has the plague. That's a pest house. Let's get away from here!"

As his voice faded in the distance, Hal crept along the floor until she found the package he had thrown. "Food!" she cried. "Food!"

No banquet had ever tasted better. There was cold chicken, bread, a few radishes, a large hunk of cheese, two cucumbers and a small head of lettuce. Sitting close together on the floor in the dark they ate it, using their fingers. Suddenly they felt strong again and eager for dawn. As they listened, it became clear that the fighting had, indeed, moved away from their immediate neighborhood.

"I ask God to forgive me for doubting Him," said George humbly.

"If I ever meet that Roundhead again," said Mary, "I will make him an earl."

Several hours later when they were growing drowsy again, the door opened and someone whispered, "Your Majesty?"

"Jeffrey Hudson?" asked the Queen. "Is it you?"

"Yes, your Majesty, and the Countess of Carlyle and the Duke of Hurley is with me."

"*Comment!* How did you find us?"

"We were the last to leave Bedford House," said the Duke, "and we've been wandering around, lost, trying to avoid the fighting since dawn. Then about an hour ago a young Roundhead stopped us and quickly told us where to find you. At first we were afraid to come, thinking it a trap."

"We managed to buy some food," said the dwarf.

Mary laughed, a short, nervous laugh. "We'll keep it for the journey. We have feasted. That same Roundhead—an angel with clipped hair—was our nocturnal visitor. But sit down. You must sit on the floor. We have no chairs. But—*n'importe*. We have only to wait until dawn and we start. *Quelle heure est-il?* Ah, but how can you know what time it is? Make yourselves comfortable, *mes amies*. We shall try to sleep a little."

The seven occupants of the cabin lapsed into silence. Presently the Duke began to snore. Hal relaxed against the wall, no longer fearful. Jerry—bless him!—was watching over her, strong, vigilant and resourceful. It was a lovely feeling, this feeling of being loved and cared for. She let herself dream blissfully of the time when the land would be at peace, its ugly wounds healing, and she and Jerry would find each other, no longer isolated by two separate worlds, but coming together joyously and normally to live —as in the tales Cheam had told her in her childhood— happily ever after.

Delightful visions like this could make her oblivious to the Queen's low moans, the snores of the Duke, the restless stirring of the dwarf, the heat of the unclean, airless shack. She was sure that she had not slept at all when through the small, grimy window she discerned the first faint streak of gray.

She awakened her companions and when they had eaten, George cautiously opened the door. Except for a stray cat, the street was empty. He motioned to his companions, and Hal, with the aid of the priest, assisted Mary to rise.

They had three miles to go before reaching the now unguarded gate of the city, seven shabby people who had to move slowly because of the woman in the midst of them with the pallid, pain-wracked face. They did not speak, for even speech required strength; but many of them were praying.

"Dear Lord," begged Hal, "thank you for helping us this far. Please—oh, please, don't let the Queen die or faint. Keep us going, Lord; just—keep us going!"

They did keep going and nobody noticed them. The town was coming to life now but it had more to think about than seven people trudging along in the sun. In almost every building there was someone wounded, or there were windows to be repaired or crying children to be pacified.

Once outside the gate, the refugees remembered that their benefactor had instructed them to take the road to the right. It was a long, rural road, sunny, dusty and hot. The women, unaccustomed to such heavy shoes, were already limping. The men, unshaven, took turns in half-carrying the Queen. Evidences of war were everywhere. The road was littered with bodies of men and horses.

Now and then parties of other refugees passed the bedraggled royal entourage, mostly with loaded carts, and the Queen's party choked in the dust. At noon when they came to a farmhouse they sank to the earth in the shade of a tree while George sought the goodwife, offering to buy milk and food.

When he returned she was with him, he carrying the milk, she carrying what food she could spare.

"Refugees from Exeter—" she was saying, "there's a lot of 'em today. Must've been bad there. Sorry I can't spare you more food. I hear the Queen's in Exeter but the soldiers haven't found her. Poor woman. My man says she don't deserve no pity. He says if we could just get our hands on 'er, Parliament would give us such a big reward that we'd be rich."

They wanted to get rid of the woman, and the Countess, forgetting her disguise, spoke haughtily.

"That's all, thank you, my good woman. You may go now."

Instantly, the housewife bristled. "Who do you think you are, talkin' to me like that? I'm as good as you are!"

"My mother apologizes," said Hal quickly. "You must please excuse her. She's tired and edgy and her feet hurt."

The woman was pacified. "Hurtin' feet—that'll make a person edgy, all right. What's the matter with that one?" she pointed to the Queen.

Mary did not dare to speak, knowing that her accent would betray her.

"She's not well," replied Hal. "Rather faint, but she'll

be all right. She's my aunt. I'll take care of her. We haven't much farther to go—only to Lydford."

"You're lucky it ain't rainin'," said the sturdy, round-faced farm woman. "Well, I can't stand here talkin'. I got a lot to do." She hurried back to the house.

"Whew!" George said, sinking to the ground. "I thought she'd never go. I'm famished. Quick thinking, to say we were going to Lydford. In case they should try to trace us."

They served the Queen first, but without ceremony, and when the rest of them had eaten, they gazed at the long road ahead, reluctant to rise from this cool, shady place under the kindly oak.

"Your Majesty is very tired—" began Hal.

"*Point du tout,*" replied Mary with a hint of her characteristic spirit. "Come, let's move on. Where does this road lead? Are you sure it will take us to Plymouth?"

"It will take us to Lydford and Princetown and then almost straight to Plymouth," replied George. "The woman told me as she fixed the food. We aren't lost." He was assisting the Queen to rise, and the others circled protectively around her, making sure she was in the center of them so that they could defend her if the necessity arose.

The road was quiet now, and free of corpses. Some dogs ran toward them, barking ferociously, but they backed off when the Duke threw a stone at them. A woman milking a goat looked up idly as they passed, and some men who were shearing sheep called out, "Is Exeter in the hands of the Roundheads?"

"Yes," answered George.

"Where's the King?"

"I don't know."

They moved on. Mary, her voice breaking pathetically,

echoed the question. "Where is the King? Ah, if I knew!"

That night they thought it best to make camp off the road instead of asking shelter at a farmhouse, where the Queen's accent would surely betray them. They found a place near a stream where they washed and drank deep of the cool water. Several of the men killed pigeons which, when the women had plucked them, they roasted over a small fire. Hal found some cress in the stream. The food was insufficient to satisfy their hunger, but it was better than nothing, and, Hudson and George being elected to keep watch, the others fell into restless sleep.

At dawn they were on their way again, the women's dresses crumpled and soiled, their mouths tense with anxiety, their faces drawn with weariness. The chief concern of all of them was that the Queen might collapse at any moment. Now and then she would groan softly, muttering, "How warm it is!"

It was dusk when they reached the hut in the woods, a place so hidden by trees that they had to look sharply to find it. There were deep sighs of relief. Here they were to wait for the rest of their party. There was a well, but the place was empty except for a few rickety chairs, some broken pottery and a large pot near the fireplace. The women collected wood and made a fire. The men killed some larks and rabbits which they stewed in the pot, along with some wild carrots Hal found.

Next morning their friends began to arrive, coming in threes and fours. Fortunately, some of them brought food.

It was not far now to Plymouth. Not joining in the conversation of the others, Hal sat apart from them, thinking. Where could the Queen go after reaching that seaport? What more natural haven then France where her brother was king?

Which side was winning? It was impossible to tell. The vague reports stressed alternating victories. Certainly up to now the Parliamentary forces had not been particularly aggressive, but a change in leadership had recently taken place.

One of the Puritan leaders, now dead, a man named Hampden, had a cousin who was becoming more and more active in the war—a former member of Parliament now in his mid-forties, an ill-groomed man with a straight, cruel mouth named Oliver Cromwell.

He and his cavalry had fought splendidly at Newark last year, but he had been repulsed at Gainsborough. In October there had been another battle at Wincey when Colonel Cromwell's horse had been shot from under him. But he had mounted another and fought on, finally driving back the King's forces. His men were now beginning to be called "Cromwell's Ironsides." He was rapidly superceding Essex, for Essex, after all, was a noble and as such was loth to be overly active against his King.

The troops of Essex had been scattered everywhere, but now Cromwell was welding them into a formidable force. It was said that Charles held mastery in the west and held Bristol, the second city in the kingdom, but his forces had met with a repulse at Gloucester.

Actually, although the small band of Royalists did not know it, Charles was fighting his way toward his wife, determined to reach her, but he had to contend with enemy forces for every mile of his advance. At that very moment he was moving toward Exeter.

Sitting in the cabin that night, Hal knew she must reach a decision. Having surmised that once in Plymouth Mary would be unable to move anywhere except across the sea, she faced that possibility with concern. The motto of her house was "Duty and Loyalty." But now where was her duty, where was her loyalty? If the Queen left England was it her duty to go, too? Did not loyalty make this imperative? But suddenly there was another loyalty, another duty —loyalty to love, duty to herself and the man she loved.

An argument, long and intense, took place within her. Finally she made up her mind. If the Queen went to France she would not accompany her. She would stay and find Jerry.

Having arrived at this decision she rose and went outside, seeking her brother who with several other men was holding guard around the hut. It was a mild June night and George was seated on the grass. She sank beside him.

"Peace seems the most desirable thing in the world," he said moodily. "Just peace. Think how many Englishmen have already been killed in this war! Englishmen fighting each other. How I hate it!"

"I, too; but I didn't come to talk about that. When the Queen gets to Plymouth she'll surely decide to go to France."

"Yes, I've thought of that. It would be the wise thing to do. Where else could she go?"

"You'll go with her, I suppose?" she asked wistfully.

"Of course. How could we desert her now? And France seems alluring, for there we could exist in peace and safety. Yes, if she chooses to go to France, we'll certainly accompany her. She trusts us and depends on us."

"I shall not go," she answered firmly.

"What? What did you say?"

"I shall not go to France."

"But it's your——"

"I know. You're going to remind me of my duty. For hours I've been struggling over that. My heart is here,

George. I love the Queen, but I love someone else more."

"I order you to go to France! I'm responsible for you. How could I leave you here, all alone and practically penniless?"

"First I'd try to find Jerry. If I couldn't, then I'd try to find Cheam. Odd, I still think of her as Cheam. She's at Budleigh Salterton."

"Don't be silly. That's on the channel, not too far from Exeter. How would you get there?"

"If necessary, walk."

"That's impossible. No one to look after you."

"I'm learning to take care of myself. Besides, I still have some of the money left of what Cheam returned to me. So at night I wouldn't have to sleep in the open."

"Be sensible, Hal. You can't do this. Be patient. The war will end sometime and then we'll come back and——"

"I'm not going to France, George," she insisted.

"I say you shall! Our duty is to the King and his family!"

"You can't force me to go and I hope you won't try. The Queen might command me to go, but for the first time in my life I shall disobey her. My duty and my loyalty belong first to the man I love and there's nothing you or anyone else can do about that!"

10 ❀

the rebel

AT DAYBREAK THE QUEEN AND HER PARTY LEFT THE HUT.
Though still weak, her Majesty had less pain in her legs,
and now that Plymouth was so close and anxiety for their
safety had dwindled, it seemed to those who tended her
that she was much stronger than when they had escaped
from Exeter.

It was a sorry-looking band that found refuge in Plymouth at Pendennis Castle, but now the refugees could
bathe and dine and relax, for Plymouth was a royal fortress.
London was two hundred and forty-seven miles away.
There was still fighting going on on the outskirts of Exeter
and this made the enemy seem perilously close.

The day after their arrival the royal party gathered in
Mary's sitting room. The men had shaved, and though they
still wore their rough, homespun garments their collars
and cuffs had been washed, starched and ironed, they had
put on their rings and they had been able to buy swords.

Some of the ladies had packed dresses in their bundles.
These gowns had been pressed. Their coiffures were smart

and they wore their jewels. Hal was still in the brown dress, but she had discarded her soiled kerchief and apron.

Outwardly all of them seemed serene and poised. They were excessively polite to one another and observed the required subservience to the Queen; but inwardly they were all undergoing the same keen insecurity. Exeter, once having been a Royalist garrison, had been compelled to surrender to the Roundheads. Who knew but that Plymouth might be next? This fear was uppermost in their minds.

From Plymouth, only the sea offered any hope of escape. They were weary of wandering, weary of trudging in the sun, weary of dust. The general thought was, "I could never, never go through that again!"

But what they did and where they went depended upon one person, the Queen. She was their leader and she was also their burden, for at all hazards they must protect her and care for her, yet they must obey her. How long could they stay in Plymouth? And after Plymouth—what?

They were reluctant to voice these queries to her Majesty. It was for her to decide. They must wait for her to speak. Meanwhile they smiled at each other and in calm, well-bred voices discussed impersonal things, such as what a pleasant day it was, how fresh and invigorating was the sea air, and how, back in the days of Elizabeth, Sir Francis Drake had sailed from yonder port, and wasn't Plymouth a delightful town? So clean, so busy, and the shops were really quite nice.

Mary took no part in this idle conversation.

Looking exhausted and white, she was seated in an armchair gazing out thoughtfully over the harbor. Her hostess had been able to supply her with several gowns and a maid had arranged her black hair in its usual shiny curls.

"Hudson—" she said.

Her faithful dwarf bounded toward her. "Madam?"

"In the harbor is a Dutch ship. See her pennant?"

"I see it, your Majesty."

"So. *Ça va.* Go talk to the captain. Tell him that the Queen of England wishes to take refuge from her enemies in the kingdom of her brother, Louis of France. Say that she has with her a small suite. Can he—will he transport them to some French port? And when? How soon can he sail? *Me comprenez-vous?*"

"Yes, your Majesty."

When the dwarf left the room, moving quickly on his short legs, Mary turned to her women and officers, addressing each singly.

"You, Monsieur le Duc, will sail with me?"

One after the other, some with a slight hesitation, the men and women nodded. A few were delighted at the thought of reaching some place where they would find respite from suspense and danger, others thought longingly of their families, but like Hal and her brother they had been schooled from babyhood to be faithful to the crown.

"You, my Lord George? You will come. *Cela va sans dire.* That goes without saying."

"Wherever I may serve the Queen's Grace," he replied with a gallant bow. *"Cela va sans dire."*

"And you, Hal?" she smiled fondly. "But I know I need not even ask."

"Your Majesty," answered Hal gravely, "I cannot go."

There were gasps of astonishment. The Queen's eyes brightened with surprise.

"Comment! What is the matter? You're joking."

"I—I'm sorry, but—I must refuse to accompany your Majesty."

160

"Why?"

"Because—because my heart is here. I am wondrously in love."

"What matter? I command you, come with me!"

"Madam, forgive me," begged Hal miserably. "I cannot."

"What! You would desert me? Who has heard of such a thing? In love! With that Roundhead? *Fi donc!* Your poor *maman!* God rest her soul. She would blanch at the idea of a Royalist marrying a Roundhead. Don't dissappoint me, Hal."

"Your Majesty knows what love is," said Hal pleadingly. "You are leaving the man you love because circumstances force you to do so, but your heart must be torn at the thought."

"Yes," Mary admitted. Then, after a brief pause, "You must love this Roundhead very much."

"I do. Oh, I do! Forgive me if this appears as disloyalty."

The spectators were frowning, shocked at Hal's unwillingness to sacrifice her love for the royal cause. Mary's voice was cold, and Hal realized how much she had hurt this woman who had been so fond of her.

"I am grateful for what you and yours have done for me. I shall not stand in the way of so great a love." Mary sighed. "I am parted from my husband and children. I know the pangs of separation. *Tiens!*" Her voice was sarcastic now. "I wish you well. *Je vous félicite.*"

"Oh, madam, thank you!" Hal's eyes filled with tears. "But don't be angry with me. My family has given everything to the royal cause. Our home is gone, our fortune is gone, and I—oh, madam, I would gladly go on giving everything—everything except my love! And yet, for all I know he might have been killed at Exeter or perhaps lies wounded and suffering!"

"That you would marry a Roundhead! Who would have believed it!"

"Let me remind your Majesty that this Roundhead probably saved your life, not once but twice."

"He did not do it to protect me, but to save you. Had it not been for your presence with me he would have been glad to have taken me a prisoner to London and receive the big reward." She turned to George. "My lord, did you know of this fool's resolve?"

"She announced it to me one night when we were in the forest, madam."

"And you would sail away, leaving her unprotected?"

"It is sometimes a struggle, madam, to know where one's duty lies. All our lives my sister and I, being the sole surviving children of our parents, have been very close. Now she has made this foolish decision. What can I do about it? I can only respect the fact that God has given to her as to us all a certain precious thing called free will. Yes, madam, I, too, have free will, and it is by my own free will that I continue to serve you, as I have sworn to do, if you need me."

She turned to Hal, eyes flashing angrily. "Would you dare to wed without my consent?"

"I beg you not to withhold it, madam; but—yes, I shall marry the one my heart guides me to. Indeed, I haven't even my father's consent, but even so, I shall not hesitate."

The Queen sighed, no longer incensed. "So great a love," she muttered, not sarcastic now, but filled with wonderment.

There was a deep silence in the room. Mary turned her gaze toward the harbor, her black eyes pools of worriment. Was her going a wise thing? But what else could she do?

She often referred to herself as the unhappiest queen on earth and never had she been more miserable than now.

Everyone avoided looking at Hal and she knew that these people who had been her friends were friends no longer.

At last the silence was broken by the entrance of Hudson, panting from heat and exertion.

"Well?" asked the Queen impatiently.

The dwarf reported that the Dutch captain would receive Mary and her party, but that he must sail at dawn next morning.

"Très-bien, je vous remercie. I wonder where the King is. Oh, if I knew how things were going with my lord! I wish to be alone. *Allez-vous-en."*

They knelt and left the room. Once in the hall, pointedly ignoring Hal, they went to their rooms intent upon writing to their loved ones and sending the letters by a messenger of the castle. Hal, depressed because her decision had alienated her from her friends and hurt the Queen, made her way to the kitchen. She was filled with sorrow at the thought of parting from her brother, but knowing that France was safer than England she said to herself, "If he stays here he's likely to be killed."

The bag of gold Nancy had given her was now about three-quarters filled, and she used some of the money to pay the chef to prepare a substantial bundle of food, enough to last until she reached Exeter.

Though Budleigh Salterton could be more quickly reached by a short cut from Plymouth she decided to return to Exeter in the hope that there she might find Jerry. Though she knew the way, she had never traveled alone before and the prospect was frightening.

Having made arrangements with the chef she went to

the room that had been allotted to her, and paid one of the maids to give her a shampoo and supply her with a new set of clothes.

She felt fresh and clean as she sat in the sun drying her hair. Of course, Jerry might not be still at Exeter and she might have some difficulty in finding him. Once she reached there, Lady Morton would receive her graciously and might be able to help her.

Presently she saw her brother striding toward her. His old flirtatiousness and carefree attitude were gone. He was no longer boyish. There were tense wrinkles about his well-shaped mouth and his eyes were grave.

"Are you still determined to let us go without you?" he asked, sinking to the lawn beside her. "I suppose you realize that you're being extremely foolish."

"Perhaps."

"And if the Queen should return to England you'll never again be appointed to serve her."

"I know. I have forfeited her friendship. But George, do you think she'll ever return? Every day that this fighting continues the people grow more and more resentful of the King, and in spite of all that money and materiel the Queen brought from Holland he can't claim any outstanding victories."

"News has just come that he's trying to get to Exeter, but his forces are compelled to fight every step of the way. He's said to be only about twenty miles outside it. Oh, Hal, I feel terrible, going off and leaving you. Have you any money? I can't give you any, you know."

"As I told you I still have the bag Nancy gave me. There's plenty to last until I reach her. Have you heard anything from Father?"

"Nothing." He gazed at her thoughtfully. "You've

changed a great deal since those days at Langdon Hall."

"I know. I no longer think as I did then. How silly, how snobbish I was! I imagined that because I was of the gentry God had made me superior to working people. Well, I'm wiser now. Instead of looking down on them, I admire them. And another thing, I no longer believe that all power should be in the hands of one man, such as a king. 'Give me liberty to know, to think, to believe, and to utter freely according to conscience.' That's a quotation from Milton. And I'm sure he's right. I want England to be a country where all people have liberty to believe and think according to their conscience. I think all men should have this right, and I think in the end the right must prevail."

"In other words you think the King's cause is lost."

"Yes, George. Yes, I do. He's a valiant, noble man, but I no longer think as the Queen does that just because he's a king he's infallible. I believe that never again in England will a king have absolute power."

"You may be right, but right or wrong, I wish things were settled! Now let's talk about you. When you get to Exeter you'll surely go to Lady Morton, but—oh, Hal, I wish you weren't so stubborn! You've never been that way before."

"That's because I've never been in love before. I know I belong with Jerry. This is the most important thing in my whole life."

"Are you sure you'd feel that way if things were as they used to be and he had no money?"

"Of course. Jerry is rich in other, more important ways —rich in intelligence, in courage, in kindness. You know, George, among the commoners a woman often refers to her husband as 'my man.' Well, Jerry Vane is my man and nothing will ever change that."

"I can only wish you luck. Well, there's a messenger leaving tomorrow with letters. I want to get one off to Father. Whew! Wait till he hears what you're doing! He'll be ashamed to hold up his head when he learns that you've abandoned the Queen!" He walked away angrily.

Supper, served in the great hall that night, was a silent meal, and Mary dismissed the company early, having pointedly ignored Hal, an attitude reflected by the others.

At sunrise they were dressed, and after a hearty breakfast, ready to start. Hal followed them to the ship, prepared to begin her own long journey, carrying two bundles —the bag of money and the food.

George kissed her. "I'll come back when the Queen gives me leave. Meanwhile, all I can do is place you in God's hands. The governor of Pendennis Castle said he couldn't spare you a horse or an escort."

"I didn't expect him to. Good-by, George, and don't worry about me. Write when you can—in care of Nancy."

"Yes. Good-by."

He strode up the gangplank, not looking back. Some of the others passed her, a few with averted eyes, others with chilly *adieux*. At the gangplank Mary turned to her coldly and Hal's eyes filled with tears, for she had a premonition that she would never see this woman again.

"It's not too late to change your mind, my lady."

"I—I'm sorry, madam. God take care of you!"

"Adieu."

Hal knelt. "Farewell, your Majesty."

Queen Mary walked up the gangplank.

Looking little and defenceless, holding her bundles, dressed in a clean, wine-colored, badly-fitting dress, Hal stood watching the boat as it took her friends away. No one except George waved to her from the rail. She waved

166

at him brightly, though her vision was blurred by tears, and she felt suddenly frightened at her aloneness.

When the ship was out of sight, she turned, walking quickly along the cobbled, crowded street, and presently the town was behind her. On its outskirts she came upon a group of children playing with stilts. They alone seemed unmindful of the long, brutal war. A little farther on a man was mowing buckwheat, while a few farm women were picking and drying flax. To them she looked like a pretty serving maid as she smiled shyly at them.

"Have a peach?" asked one of the women.

"Why, thank you. Thank you very much. It looks delicious. I was really thirsty."

"Stop a while, then, and have a mug of cider."

"You're very kind."

They gave her the cider and when she had drained the mug she handed it back, explaining that she was on her way to Exeter.

"It's a long way, mistress."

"Yes, I know."

"What's the news? Where's the Queen? We heard she'd gone to Plymouth. Odd, we didn't see her pass. No fanfares or anything. It must be a lie."

"No. She was in Plymouth, but she sailed for France."

"Did she now? Well, good riddance. And where's the King, would you know that?"

"I heard he hadn't yet reached Exeter."

"Why are you going there if there's to be more fighting?"

Hal's smile widened. "I'm going to be married," she announced proudly as she took to the road again.

"I'm going to be married." It was like a refrain, echoing and re-echoing in her mind.

Had she been downcast because she had bade farewell to

her friends? But the world was full of friends! It had been a friendly hand that had given her the cider and the sweet, juicy peach. She gazed at several jackdaws who were regarding her solemnly from a fence rail.

"I'm going to be married," she told them, but they took wing and flew away, not comprehending this glorious announcement.

Presently she began to feel tired and she seated herself in the shade of a tree, opening her bundle of food. Except for the cawing of the rooks and the sharp, piercing yell of a yaffle everything was silent around her. The sky was a pale, cloudless blue and no breeze stirred the leaves in the tall trees.

The thought of Langdon Hall came to her, and she saw again the beautiful stained glass windows in the chapel, the great hall with its dark, oak-paneled walls gleaming like satin; the Christmas festivities, the snow outside, the lively fire on the hearth, and Jerry entering with his grandmother through the door at the far end. That was Christmas, 1641, and now it was July, 1644. How scornful and resentful she had been of his clipped hair then—and yet his presence had stirred her in a strange way. She thought she must have fallen in love with him that day, though she had stubbornly refused to admit it.

"Dear Lord," she prayed, "help me to find him!"

She remembered the reunion of Charles and Mary in the Vale of Keinton—so moving, so tender; and the hopefulness of the Royalists during their stay at Oxford. How suddenly it had changed!

She thought of that unexpected meeting with Jerry in the rushes near the Avon and how content she had felt sitting there, her hand in his. Why was she dawdling here by the side of the road? Something might be happening to him this very minute! Swiftly, she tied the large bundle of food and rose, eager to be on her way again. She had not gone far when she saw a band of Roundheads coming toward her. It was easy to recognize them because of their scarfs, high-crowned hats, loose, plain coats and long swords.

She gazed about, seeking for some place to hide, for she had heard that Cromwell's men had been known to massacre women. In the distance were several small cottages with wooden shutters, but they were too far off for shelter. Then, behind her, she saw a ruined brick wall almost hidden by yew trees. She ran toward it and flung herself down behind it.

The men were talking earnestly but she could hear nothing except something about Marsten Moor, something about Fairfax and Cromwell and the Scots against Prince Rupert. This, she surmised, meant an impending battle on Marsten Moor, a place well to the north, between York and Knaresborough. If the Parliamentarians were assembling around Marsten Moor in vast numbers, perhaps Jerry had gone there! This was a disconcerting thought and long after the men had passed she lingered behind the wall, considering it.

Then she realized that the sky was darkening alarmingly and the leaves of the trees were restlessly showing their undersides, which foretold a storm.

Quickly she picked up her bundles, hurrying along the road, while the increasing wind made swirls of dust and tore at her skirts. The storm broke just as she reached the forest, a furious downpour, with thunder shaking the earth and lightning tearing erratically through the darkened sky. The farmers welcomed it, since there had been a long, dry spell, but to Hal, plodding along alone, it was a terrifying experience.

In five minutes she was wet to the skin. Her feet, in their heavy-soled, ugly shoes sloshed through mud that before half an hour was almost up to her ankles. She struggled on, hunched, sliding, her almost-blinded eyes alert for the cabin in the woods. When finally she reached it, grateful for its shelter, she sank weakly to the dirt floor.

The storm lasted for two days—days when seemingly the small house would be shattered by the wind. There was a leak in the roof, so Hal was confined to one small corner, the only dry spot. Knowing that the storm must reach the sea, she was worried about her brother and the Queen.

Suspecting that a great battle might even now be going on at Marsten Moor, she trembled for the safety of Jerry and her father. Wet and miserable, with the hem of her dress caked with mud, she sat through the dragging hours, occasionally drifting off to sleep, and quoted passages from the Bible to divert her mind from the war and the lightning. Eating some of the food, she saw that she must now put herself on rations.

When at last the wind died down, the rain continued, dismally and doggedly. The fearful storm ended on the morning of the third day, but eager as Hal was to leave that lonely cabin she knew that it would be impossible to proceed until the roads had a chance to dry.

The following morning she started off, though even now scarcely anyone but herself would venture on the road. The mud was still deep and slippery, forcing her to move slowly and cautiously. She knew she was a disreputable-looking creature, what with her dress all wrinkled and her shoes mud-caked.

Exeter seemed much, much farther away than she remembered it. All morning she walked. At noon there was a brief stop for lunch, then back to the endless road again.

Finally from behind her she heard the creak of a cart. It moved slowly, making deep ruts in the mire and when it came abreast of her she saw that in the driver's seat was a middle-aged, bald-headed man and his buxom wife who were taking produce to Exeter. The woman asked if she wanted a ride and she happily nodded. Staunchly for Parliament, they took it for granted that she was, too, and their conversation focused upon this man Cromwell upon whom, it seemed, all their hopes were resting. The woman sharply announced that she loathed "them Cavaliers."

"Have you ever seen Cromwell?" Hal asked. "What's he like?"

"Pious chap," answered the man, "with a long nose, hair parted in the middle, forehead always wrinkled in a frown. A Puritan. Not a man you'd take to. 'Everything that happens,' he says, 'is the work of God.' What's your name, lass, and where d'you come from?"

"From Plymouth. My name's Henrietta Wade."

"Named for the Queen, were you? Where is that she-devil now?"

"I—I heard she'd escaped to France. Sir, do you know where the King is? Is he at Marsten Moor?"

"They say he's somewhere around Exeter. It's in the hands of the Ironsides now and he intends to take it—if he can."

"Were you in the war?" asked Hal.

"That I was. Wounded fighting under Colonel Cromwell. At Newark it was, on the Lincolnshire border. Every day, seemed like, there'd be a skirmish with them Royalists. Once at Wincey, that was last year in October, the Colonel's horse was shot from under him. I seen it with my own eyes. But nothing feezes Ol' Ironsides."

"You wouldn't happen to know, would you, a fellow

named Jerry Vane? Dark hair. Tall. With a wondrously friendly smile and friendly dark eyes?"

"No," replied the man thoughtfully, "don't recollect anyone by that name, but the way you describe him I'd say you was in love with him."

Hal beamed unashamedly. "That's why I'm going to Exeter—to find him."

"Parliament's army is large, you know," said the woman. "You wouldn't be thinking of following him in the war, would you? I'd advise against it. Lots of women follow their men, but if you was my daughter I wouldn't let you."

They were silent for a time, then the woman, looking down at Hal's small hands, spoke suspiciously. "Maybe we've taken you as far as we've a mind to. You don't look like a farm lass and those hands're too white ever to have known the sting of hot starch and too soft to've touched a churn; and those pretty fingernails, I'll warrant, never dug into the earth. You know what I think you are? You're a Royalist!"

"I—I was an embroiderer at Pendennis Castle and I used to do some stitchery for Lady Morton at Exeter."

The woman still seemed antagonistic.

"But now," went on the girl quietly, "there's only one thought in me—to find my man and to love him, love him till I die."

Immediately the antagonism vanished. "Aye," said the woman feelingly, gazing at the insignificant-looking man in the leather breeches, "it's myself that knows how you feel, lass."

And suddenly, there in the heavy mist that began to fill the midsummer twilight, these two strangers were strangers no longer. They were women knowing what love meant, and love had made them one. When half an hour later they parted at the town gate they felt as though they had known one another for a long, long time.

Hal walked down a narrow street of gray stone houses. Soldiers carrying rushlights strolled along, some with girls. They seemed carefree, like victors, and they paid scant attention to the slender, frowsy lass who hurried along as though she had been sent on some errand. A group of young people stood watching a puppet show, its small characters lighted by several candles. In a little shop a linen-draper still labored, intent upon finishing an order. On the front step of a tiny, whitewashed dwelling an old woman sat, dully watching the movement in the street.

Hurrying along, Hal looked hopefully into every face, but the one she sought was not among them. During that walk to Exeter there had been times when she thought that it would be easy to find him, that the mighty presence of God had her by the hand and would lead her directly to him.

Arriving at Morton House she was pleasantly received.

"Lady Hal!" exclaimed her hostess. "What are you doing here? Don't tell me you traveled alone?"

"Yes. May I ask shelter for the night?"

"Of course. Of course. You're welcome to stay as long as you like, but where's the Queen? Why have you left her?"

"She has gone to France."

"And you didn't go with her? Why?"

"I—I came back because—because"—she hesitated, knowing how horrified Lady Morton would be at this disclosure—"well, because I'm in love with a soldier and he's a Roundhead and I hoped he was in Exeter and I want to find him. Please, may I buy some fresh clothes from one of your maids? And could I purchase one of your horses?"

"There's an old one, not good for anything. You may have her, and you certainly need some fresh clothes. You must be hungry, too. I'll ring for food. But, your ladyship, do you mean to say that you have abandoned the Queen for no other reason except to find a soldier? A Roundhead? You mean that you'd marry him?"

"If I find him and he asks me."

"Well! By my soul! This is the wildest thing I ever heard of! A lady of your position confessing that she's hunting for a man—and a Roundhead! What has the war done to you? Why, this is positively scandalous!"

"I know," admitted Hal meekly.

"You'd go off unattended, unchaperoned. You'd associate with all sorts of ruffians and traitors. Indeed, my lady, it seems you've taken leave of your senses!"

"I know your ladyship thinks it shocking, but to me it seems a natural thing to do."

"Suppose you don't find him in Exeter?"

"Then I shall go to the Duchess of Thewes at Budleigh Salterton."

"I heard about that. Imagine the Duke marrying a woman who was so far beneath him, who inveigled him into——"

"There was no inveigling. He was grateful to her for taking care of him when he was ill. I've known the Duchess all my life. She's one of the finest persons I've ever met and I'll ask you not to think or say anything wrong about her. It was the Duke who insisted on the marriage. I was there and I know. Now tell me, where's the King?"

"Only about fifteen—twenty miles from here, they say. As you know, the Roundheads have taken the town. They came here searching for the Queen. They saw the little

Princess—that poor mite who hasn't been named yet—but the servants and I swore the child was mine. So the Roundheads went away and did no harm. Oh, isn't it dreadful what happened at Marsten Moor?"

"What happened?"

"There was a terrible battle. They say the Royalists were about thirty-five thousand strong under Prince Rupert. There were about twenty-four thousand Parliamentarians and Scots. Our side was completely beaten. Three thousand of our men were left dead on the field."

"Oh!"

"Old Ironsides, whom they call Cromwell now, took much Royalist artillery and one thousand five hundred prisoners. York has surrendered. It's a crushing blow to the cause of Charles I—crushing!"

"How dreadful! Is all Yorkshire gone?"

Lady Morton nodded.

"How can the King recover from a defeat like that?" asked Hal. "Can he? I doubt it."

The attitude of her hostess was no longer friendly, and Hal understood why. What she had done—abandoning the Queen and rushing off unchaperoned to find a man, especially a Roundhead—was nothing short of disgraceful. She had known beforehand that she would have to face this reaction among her own set.

Lady Morton showed her to her room and left her. A few minutes later her supper was served on a small table. Having eaten, she ordered some warm water to soak her sore and swollen feet. The maid brought a dark gray dress and asked if it would do. Hal smiled and said it would do very well. Then she went to bed to fall at once into a sound, dreamless sleep.

It was late morning when she awakened. She dressed and pulled the bell cord for breakfast, which was brought in by a maid followed by her hostess.

"Good morning, my lady," said Hal cheerily.

Lady Morton did not smile. Her voice was frigid. "May I ask how your ladyship proposes to go about finding this Roundhead?"

"What can I do but make inquiries? Someone must know him."

"I shan't permit it. It's the most shocking thing I ever heard of."

"You can hardly stop me, my lady."

"Think of your reputation. Think of the humiliation you're bringing to your poor father."

"I would rather think of my happiness."

"I ought to lock you up to prevent you from making a disgrace of yourself!"

"I'm leaving this morning, my lady. I thank you for the horse. One of your maids has supplied me with this dress and food for the journey. I know in your eyes I'm a rebel, but these are not normal times, my lady. Your position, my position—these are no longer secure; nor, for a matter of fact, is life itself. There's war in the streets, there's war in the fields. There's pride and hatred and bloodshed, but above everything there's love, and love—at least to me—seems the most precious and the most important thing of all."

"You are the greatest fool in the kingdom," said Lady Morton as she left the room, "but I must admit you have courage!"

11

the search

It was late when Hal started out on that sultry July day, for she first visited the nursery where the nameless wee princess was sleeping. Then, looking fresh and trim in her charcoal gray dress, she went down into the courtyard where a groom was holding a somewhat woebegone-looking mare. In the saddlebags Hal put her bundle of food, the bag of money and another package containing some things she had bought from the maid—a comb, a towel, a washcloth, an additional set of underwear, a second pair of coarsely-knitted hose, and a cape with a hood.

Today her ladyship did not ride in the elegant, aristocratic way, using a sidesaddle, but astride the animal as did the peasant women. Riding slowly out of the paved courtyard, she wondered how to begin her search. Turning east, she presently entered the business thoroughfare, still moving slowly, eyes alert, expecting to meet him at any moment.

The siege being over, people were going about their business in a normal way. There were women with large market baskets, soldiers lounging about or on horseback, children playing. It was not long before she passed the Seven Stars, an inn, where many people, mostly soldiers, were entering and leaving, while others lounged against the wall and several were seated on benches.

She decided that this must be some sort of headquarters, and so she tied the horse to a post and entered. The reception room was crowded. At one end, seated behind a long table with disordered stacks of papers in front of them, sat two men. Before them a line had formed consisting of a few old men, some soldiers and several women.

Hal took her place at the end. As each person approached the table he gave the Puritan rallying cry, thus stressing at the outset that he was friendly to the cause: "God with us. For God and the liberties of England."

Some wanted to know if the road to some place where they wished to go was safe, a woman begged for news of her son, a soldier swore that his mother was dying in Malvern Hills and asked permission to go to see her; another reported that one of his comrades was a Royalist spy; still another declared that four soldiers were fighting at the south gate. It was two hours before Hal could approach the table.

"God with us," she said. "For God and the liberties of England."

One of the men, with a careworn, rugged face, asked in a bored voice what she wanted.

"Sirs an it please you, I am trying to find a man who is one of your group. His name is Jeremiah Vane, twenty-three years old, born in Shottery; black, wavy hair; black eyes, white teeth, tall——"

"We don't have these records, lass. Move aside. Next?"

"But, sir, who has them? Where can I go?"

"They're in the hands of Colonel Colwell."

"Oh, thank you! Where can I find him?"

"Left two days agone for York. Step aside. Next?"

Frustrated, choked with tears, Hal went into the street and mounted her horse. To follow Colonel Colwell to York was unthinkable, and so as she rode toward the north gate, whenever she saw a soldier she called out, "Sir, do you know a fellow in your army by the name of Jerry Vane?"

One after another shook their heads. Sometimes they smiled flirtatiously. "Won't I do, mistress?"

She only regarded them coldly and rode on, struggling against discouragement. It was midafternoon when, beyond the north gate, she came upon a blacksmith shop. Here she purchased food and water for the horse, and there being a bench nearby under a tree, sat down and opened her lunch bag. A middle-aged soldier came limping by, dusty and weary, and sank on the bench beside her. From the way he looked at the food she knew he was hungry and she shared some of it with him.

"Please, sir, do you know a fellow in your army by the name of Jerry Vane?" How often had she asked that identical question!

"Aye," he said, wiping the peach juice from his chin with the back of his hand. "I knew him well. Good chap—good fighter. He's dead."

"Dead! Oh, no!"

"We went out a few days agone to meet the King's forces who're headed this way. There was a skirmish. I saw him fall. He didn't get up."

"Where—where was this skirmish?"

"Can't say precisely. It was on an open road—maybe twenty miles to the north. Here now, my girl, you ain't gonna faint?"

179

"No, I—I won't faint; but—but if he were only wounded, wouldn't someone have—have picked him up and carried him to a safe place?"

"Maybe so, maybe no. We were moving fast. You grow used to the man right beside you falling in a heap with a howl."

Brokenly she tied up the food sack and moved toward the horse. Somehow she could not believe that Jerry was dead. The man didn't know for sure. He had seen him fall "in a heap with a howl," and since he didn't move, had simply assumed that he was dead.

"Dear God, no! It cannot be! Not Jerry—so vital, so strong! Not Jerry!"

The road north, the man had said, about twenty miles. Surely, Jerry had been wounded, perhaps badly. That, at least, was certain. Where did they take wounded men? She rode along at a quicker pace now, scarcely noticing where she was going. Presently she saw an elderly woman walking sluggishly toward town with a market basket on one arm.

"Ma'am an it please you, I'm looking for a wounded soldier. He was wounded a few days ago on an open road to the north. Would you know where they might have taken him?"

"My son died in this war," answered the woman bitterly. "They didn't take him nowhere. They left him there in the hot sun to die. Why should they do more for your man than they did for my son?" The woman went on without even looking up.

"Jerry, Jerry," muttered Hal as she rode along. "It can't be. I won't believe it."

But so many others had died—men young and vigorous. Why should Jerry be spared? Her head was reeling. She was in a rural district now, and seeing a woman picking vegetables near a farmhouse, she stopped and asked for a drink of water.

"You poor child. You look sick. Get down from that horse. Where do you come from? Where are you going all alone?"

Because it was good to talk to a sympathetic member of her own sex, Hal told the woman about her love for a soldier, how she had started off to find him and how she had heard that he was dead.

"What was your mother thinking of to let you go like this?" asked the woman.

"My mother is dead. My father's in the war. I can't—I just can't believe that Jerry's dead! If he's wounded, I must——"

"There. There, you can't keep on hunting. Come, behave like a normal, respectable lass. Wait till the war's over. Then if the boy's alive he'll find you."

"But I must know," Hal insisted desperately. "If he's dead I must know. If he's wounded I must help him. I can't stop now! Wait till the war is over! Will it ever be over? Who thought at the beginning that it would go on this long? The King will never give in to Parliament. He loves his country, yet he's willing to see it devastated, his people killed, and still he refuses to give in!"

"He's going to have to—in the end," said the woman grimly.

"He'll die first."

"And how do you know so much about him?"

"I—it's only what I heard."

"Well now, it's almost dusk. You'd better stay here the night. My menfolks're in the war and I'm alone. I'll make you a bed in the attic."

"Oh, thank you, but I'll be glad to pay for lodging and breakfast."

"Pay if you like. I can use the money."

In the attic that night Hal could not sleep. The place was oven-hot, but it was not the heat that made her wakeful. It was clear now that she could not go on like this indefinitely. These older women—her hostess and Lady Morton —were right. Well, she would continue along this road for about twenty-five miles. If by then she did not find Jerry or had not discovered his whereabouts, she would abandon the search and head for Budleigh Salterton.

Next morning when she had washed, eaten and saddled the horse, she stood for a moment staring down that empty, winding, shadeless road.

"Wish you wouldn't go," said her hostess. "I could use a handy lass around here; besides, there seems to be a lull in the fighting right now, but there's been plenty of trouble up that way. You'd best stay. The King and his forces ain't far off. They say he intends to take Exeter and the Roundheads don't intend to put up much of a fight for it, seeing that most of their forces are up York way."

"Thank you, but I'll go on—at least for a little longer."

"If I were your mother—well, I'll say no more. I wish you well."

So they parted, and Hal started on her lonely way again. For a time the countryside was unscarred by warfare. A signpost pointed the way to Honiton and Chard. She passed a peach orchard, a field of corn almost ready for harvesting, and a plump young woman picking cucumbers.

She stopped and asked for water for herself and her horse.

"You'd better not go much farther along this road," said the woman as she drew the water from the well.

"There's been fighting. The armies will be coming this way any minute. My man and I are trying to harvest everything that's ripe, else the soldiers'll steal it."

"I'm looking for a Roundhead soldier. A tall fellow, dark-haired, lean and strong, but wounded. Would you have seen him?"

"Lots of 'em have passed and lots of 'em answer that description. I want no dealing with Roundheads. When I see one coming, I run in the house and bolt the door."

"Well, thanks for the water."

Hal had not gone far—about five miles—when the signs of war confronted her. Gardens were ruined. Several houses had been burned. Stable doors hung open. There was not a soul in sight. Then, several miles beyond, she came upon a place where there had been a recent encounter. On both sides of the road were fields where over a hundred bodies of men and horses were motionless. Sickened, trembling, she tied her horse to a tree and forced herself to peer into the faces.

With an aching heart she thought of the women who were waiting at home and praying for these men. Her own search was futile. Heavy-hearted and sick, she did not remount but led the horse farther down the road until, turning a bend, she suddenly came upon a group of twenty Roundheads who were hurriedly digging graves. They leaned on their shovels to stare at her.

"What the devil are you doing here?" asked one of the men, a young, blond fellow with a mole on the very tip of his nose.

"She's headed for the camp of the King," exclaimed another. "Arrest her. She's a spy."

"God with us. For God and the liberties of England!" she cried. "Sirs, I swear I'm no spy."

"Take her to Colonel Lowndes."

"Oh, sir, don't delay me! I'm searching for the man I'm going to marry. I heard he was dead. Would you know, any of you? His name is Jerry Vane."

"Jerry?" asked a man who up to now had not spoken. "If she's a friend of Jerry's she's all right. I know Jerry. So, you're his sweetheart! We used to tease him because he never paid no mind to the lasses that ogled him. Now I know why. He had the most beautiful of all caring what became of him."

"Where is he?" she asked excitedly. "Where can I find him?"

"Can't say. About two weeks agone he was hurt. They took him to a doctor."

"Hurt badly?"

"Looked like it."

"He didn't die? Where is the doctor?"

"He didn't die—no. I don't know the doctor's name. I heard that Colonel Lowndes discharged him. I don't know where he is now. Where would a soldier go when he's discharged? Where but home! That is, if he can get there."

"Oh, thank God he's alive! Home. That must be Budleigh Salterton. You wouldn't happen to know which road he took?"

"No. As for you, mistress, you'd best go home yourself. Decent girls belong at home when there's a war on. If Jerry still cares, he'll find you when he gets well."

"Oh, sirs, thank you! Can you tell me the quickest way to Budleigh Salterton?"

"No, we're all strangers around here. Good luck to you, mistress."

They turned back to their spading. Hal rode on, her heart singing. Jerry was alive. She must hurry now, hurry and get to Budleigh Salterton, waiting for him as a proper bride should, decorously shielded and chaperoned. Oh, thank God!

Reaching Honiton, she found a signpost pointing to Budleigh Salterton and turned in the indicated direction. The town seemed empty. Many of the houses were destroyed. A mangy dog came out from the ruins and snarled at her. Presently leaving the ghost-village behind, she came to a high mound. Beyond this she could see a broad field where about a thousand Royalists were camping. Suddenly two soldiers leaped out from behind a holly hedge and one of them caught the bridle of her horse.

"God for Queen Mary!" cried Hal.

"What are you doing here?" demanded one of the men sternly. "Where are you going, my girl?"

"Good sir, I'm trying to get to Budleigh Salterton."

"Take the road to the left. It will bring you to Axminster, from there to Seaton, from Seaton to Sidmouth. Keep to the road from there and you'll come to Budleigh Salterton. Did you pass any Roundheads on your way here?"

"A few. They were digging graves. I——"

She broke off. Seated on her horse she was able to see over the hedge. She could survey the whole field. Some men were cleaning weapons, others polishing boots, some getting their hair trimmed, some were washing clothes in a stream; others, bandaged, were lying on cots. But what caught her attention was a tall, solitary figure with a mustache and a meticulously trimmed chin beard. The man, dejected, lonely, was seated on a rock, staring in deep thought at the ground. Not far from him, silent, brooding and shabby, stood a semi-circle of eight men, evidently waiting for him to confer with them. Among these was her father.

With a cry of joy she slipped from the horse and began to run toward that tall figure on the rock.

"The King!" she cried. "It's the King!"

One of the men tried to grab her. "Here! Come back!"

But she evaded him and ran on. Before she could greet her father, she must kneel before her king, and she did so, flinging herself on the ground before him.

"Your Majesty!"

"Odds fish," cried the Marquess. "It's Hal!"

Charles, startled by this slight, gray-clad figure which seemed to have been catapulted toward him out of no-where, raised his head and stared. Then he smiled.

"Lady Hal!"

The guards who had stopped her on the road, all flustered now, ran up to arrest her, but Charles motioned them away. He looked tired, yet strong, a soldierly figure of a man. His long hair, curling at the ends, was as immaculately dressed as though the field were the great hall at Wood-stock.

His was a face with no hint of weakness and he had a firm, well-shaped mouth. Everything about him—his voice, his figure, the way he held his head—was regal. Even the fact that he stuttered slightly did not detract from his air of royalty.

"Wh-what are you doing here, my lady? Wh-where is the Queen?"

"Sire, the Queen is now on her way to France."

He seemed astonished at this news, for to be reunited with his ailing, beloved wife was the reason he had chosen to fight in this area. His one desire had been to get to her. And now she was gone.

"G-gone, you say?" he asked, as though he found this

186

incredible. "Gone?" The news clearly distressed him. "How —how is she? Wh-when did she g-go?"

"She left Plymouth on June thirtieth, sire, aboard a Dutch ship. She seemed much improved. Sire, when you reach Exeter, go to the house of Lady Morton, for there you'll find your daughter."

"The child! A d-daughter, you say? The child is w-well?"

"Beautiful, your Majesty, a healthy, flawless baby."

Without paying any more attention to Hal, who was still kneeling, he strode toward a group of officers, and she heard him say, "We must p-push on to Exeter! At once!" Instantly a trumpet sounded and the camp became a scene of action.

The Marquess came to his daughter and the two embraced joyously. Again and again they said how wonderful it was to see each other. Hal's father looked much older than when she had last seen him, and his clothes were almost threadbare, their bright colors faded, the gilt braid tarnished.

"But what are you doing here, dressed as a scullery maid?" he asked.

She told him the whole story—how Jerry had saved the lives of the Queen and her party at Exeter; about that painful journey to Plymouth; how she had let her Majesty leave for France without her and returned to search for Jerry.

"And now I'm on my way to Thewes Castle in Budleigh Salterton. He'll be going there, too, and we'll be married."

"What? Without my consent?" He shook his head. "It's a reprehensible, disgraceful thing you've done, Hal. If I had a farthing to my name I'd disinherit you."

"Yes, sir," she answered meekly.

"But it's a brave thing, too, and I'm proud of you!"

187

She grabbed him about the neck, kissing him.

"Let me go. I'm sore displeased with you. My daughter announces to her father that she's going to be married! Odds fish. In the old days a father made such an announcement to his daughter."

"The old days and the old ways are gone, Father."

"Aye, that I know. Well, can I let you be married without your father to give you away? Oh, Hal, I'm wearied to death of this fighting! Over three years I've had of it. I'm too old for it now. Only yesterday his Majesty said as much, offering me a furlough, but I said I had no home to go to and I didn't know where my children were and so I might as well stay with him. But now—wait!"

He hurried to the King, who had mounted a sleek black horse, but who listened attentively to this aging Cavalier who had served him so faithfully. The King nodded. The Marquess knelt. Then Charles dismounted and embraced him and they parted, the King to leap upon his horse again, the Marquess walking away.

"God for Queen Mary!" shouted several of the men as they became busy getting ready to move on.

"Have at you for the King!" others cried.

Presently Hal saw her father coming toward her, leading two horses, his own mounts, along with a bundle containing his few remaining clothes. She supposed that his two personal servants had been killed.

"His Majesty has given me a long furlough, my dear," he exclaimed, joyous as a boy released from school. "Could I let my daughter travel without an escort? Let's be off, then."

They rode jauntily, their voices raised in a madrigal as they used to do at Langdon Hall. At nightfall they came to an inn.

"I haven't a penny," said the Marquess, suddenly solemn. "Do you think they'd let us sleep in the barn?"

"I've enough," she answered recklessly, "thanks to the Duchess of Thewes. We'll walk in grandly and order the best in the house, just as we used to do."

"Good. Good. I'll say I'm plain Edward Wade, a poor merchant out of Plymouth. A title, these days, sometimes becomes an uncomfortable encumbrance."

The best in the house meant a badly cooked meal and two sparsely furnished rooms, both opening on a vine-covered balcony which stretched the entire length of the half-timbered structure. Having eaten, they went to their rooms at once, and the Marquess ordered a hot bath.

Not feeling sleepy, Hal walked out on the balcony where there was a soft summer breeze. Some distance away she could see a cluster of small, placid cottages with gardens and wicket gates, and beyond them the spire of a church. Candles had been lit and shone cheerily in the small windows.

The view was lovely and peaceful and she told herself how blessed she was. Her brother was safe, her father was safe, too, and Jerry was safe. She was on her way to meet him and to be reunited with her dear Nancy.

"Oh, thank you, God, thank you!" she said, half aloud.

Next morning she found herself wide awake long before dawn and eager to be on her way again. She washed and dressed, but did not pull the cord for breakfast. Remembering the extreme tiredness of her father, she decided to let him sleep an hour longer. By the time she had dressed it was dawn, a warm, rosy dawn, throbbing with birdsong. She stepped out on the balcony again. The view was as charming as it had been last night.

From this vantage point she could view a long stretch

of road. The rising splendor of the sun spread a rose-gold glow over the scene, and Hal seemed to be enveloped in its glory. Then, trudging sluggishly along the road came the lone figure of a man with his arm in a sling. Idly, she watched him, a dusty, tattered wayfarer, with clipped dark hair, somewhat shaggy.

Then her heart skipped a beat. Could it be . . . ? That was Jerry's height, with his leanness, his long strides! Could it be? Unsure, she rushed through her room and down the stairs, running at top speed past several maids who were scrubbing the floor. Out of the door she went and on the road just as he came abreast of her, not looking up.

"Soldier," she cried merrily, almost delirious with joy, "would you do me the honor of having breakfast with me?"

He raised his head. "Hal! Am I dreaming?"

"Jerry! Oh, Jerry!"

Instantly, sobbing with emotion, she was enveloped in his one free arm. His eyes were wet, too.

"I thought you had gone to France with the Queen," he said. "Oh, my sweet, my own, my dearest! I was walking along, thinking of you, and then suddenly, out of the dawn, here you are!"

"Jerry, are you badly hurt?"

"A trifle weak, sweetheart, and they say my arm'll never fire a musket again. I'm through fighting. I was on my way to Grandmother."

"And I!"

The maids were horrified to see their guest standing in the middle of the road permitting herself to be kissed by a wounded, ragged soldier.

"And she seemed like a lady!" they said.

ABOUT THE AUTHOR

Gladys Malvern, after considerable traveling, has finally settled down in a white Colonial house with the lovely Saugatuck River flowing serenely past her back door. She has no hobbies, but her greatest joys are reading, making festive cakes with lots of gooey icing, crossword puzzles, informal entertaining, gardening, and most of all, writing books.

"I'm always amazed," she says, "when people speak of writing books as work. To me it's fascinating, rewarding, wonderful. I'm especially fortunate because I'm writing for those candid, keen-minded young adults—my favorite people. I respect them highly; I admire them heartily."